Watching Jack and the child stirred something deep inside Hailey.

Of course her maternal instincts were in high gear around Megan, but it was watching Jack that gave her the lump in her throat. He was so big he could pick Megan up with one hand, like a football. And yet he was so tender with her. Maybe out of fear, or maybe because of his good heart. Probably a combination of both.

He didn't know it, but he'd make a wonderful father. For a boy or a girl. Hailey could see the signs, and it made her wish for a crazy second that Jack could live with them permanently. Megan needed him.

And so did she.

Dear Harlequin Intrigue Reader,

The thrills never stop at Harlequin Intrigue. This month, get geared up for danger and desire in double helpings!

There's something about a mysterious man that makes him all the more appealing. In *The Silent Witness* (#565), Alex Coughlin is just such a man on assignment and undercover. But can he conceal his true feelings for Nicki Michaels long enough to catch a killer? Join Dani Sinclair and find out as she returns to FOOLS POINT.

The search for the truth is Clay Jackson's only focus—until he learns the woman he never stopped loving was keeping the biggest secret of all...a baby. See why *Intimate Secrets* (#566) are the deepest with author B.J. Daniels.

Patricia Rosemoor winds up her SONS OF SILVER SPRINGS miniseries this month. Reed is the last Quarrels brother to go the way of the altar as he enters a marriage of convenience with the one woman he thought he'd never have, in *A Rancher's Vow* (#567).

Finally, welcome multitalented author Jo Leigh as she contributes her first Harlequin Intrigue title, *Little Girl Found* (#568). She also begins a three-month bonanza of books! Look for her titles from Harlequin American Romance (June) and Harlequin Temptation (July). You won't be sorry.

Gripping tales of mystery, suspense that never lets up and sizzling romance to boot. Pick up all four titles for the total Harlequin Intrigue experience.

Sincerely,

Denise O'Sullivan
Associate Senior Editor
Harlequin Intrigue

Little Girl Found
Jo Leigh

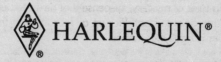

HARLEQUIN®

TORONTO • NEW YORK • LONDON
AMSTERDAM • PARIS • SYDNEY • HAMBURG
STOCKHOLM • ATHENS • TOKYO • MILAN • MADRID
PRAGUE • WARSAW • BUDAPEST • AUCKLAND

ISBN 0-373-22568-7

LITTLE GIRL FOUND

Printed in U.S.A.

ABOUT THE AUTHOR

Jo Leigh currently lives just outside Las Vegas, Nevada, where she still can't get used to the slot machines in the grocery stores. Storytelling has always been a part of her life, whether as a producer in Hollywood, a screenwriter or a novelist. It probably began when she told her third-grade teacher that elephants ate her homework.

Books by Jo Leigh

CAST OF CHARACTERS

Jack McCabe—The injured detective withdrew from the world—until a woman and child needed his protection.

Hailey Bishop—Her sexy neighbor had always seemed unapproachable. Then he showed up with a little girl in his arms and panic on his face.

Megan Chandler—The four-year-old had a secret.

Roy Chandler—Megan's father left her with the only man he knew he could trust.

Bob Dorran—Jack had to take a chance and ask for this officer's help.

Craig Faraday—The businessman knew Roy by another name. What did Roy know about him?

Crystal McCabe—Jack's dramatic ex-wife would still help him in a pinch.

Brett Nichols—Is he a cop, or a wolf in sheep's clothing?

Frank O'Neill—Would Jack's former partner turn on him?

For Paulie Rose—I love you, sweetie!

Chapter One

If the SOB said the Bulls "was robbed" one more time, Jack was going to get his gun and shoot the damn television. He should probably do it, anyway. Before, he'd never really watched it that much. A ball game here, a documentary there. But never sit-coms, and never daytime shows. He was convinced daytime television was a plot to destroy the minds of wastrels who weren't working days like good sol-diers. The only show worth a damn was *Jeopardy,* but lately he could never seem to get the final ques-tion right. Probably a sign of his diminishing mental capacity. His brain was turning to mush, just like his body.

Jack grabbed his long-necked Corona and took a swig of the warm brew. It was late, and he should go to bed. Maybe tonight he'd sleep. Maybe he wouldn't lie there in the dark, listening to the low vibrations of his downstairs neighbor's rap music, or the happy couple in 3F who liked to serenade each other with the most vile curses he'd ever heard. And that was saying something for a twelve-year veteran of the Houston PD.

And maybe tonight he wouldn't think about the way things were now. Or the way things used to be.

He got the remote from the side pocket of the recliner that had become his home and started flipping channels. Once he was away from the sports channel, it was one "infomercial" after another, each selling some contraption he didn't want or couldn't use. A potato peeler. An ab cruncher. Richard Simmons weeping in the embrace of one of his acolytes.

He kept pushing the button until he found a show in black and white. He didn't have to go further. It didn't matter what the movie was. Sighing, he tried to get comfortable again, which wasn't so easy. His hip ached, a throb that had become his constant companion. His bum leg lay unnaturally stiff, as if it was made of plastic, instead of flesh and bone.

But then he saw Richard Widmark in a wide-lapeled suit, his hat at a rakish angle and his smile as wicked as the devil's pet cat. It occurred to Jack that a fresh beer would hit the spot, and maybe a salami sandwich. But that would mean getting up. He wasn't that thirsty.

THE POUNDING ON HIS DOOR sent a jolt of adrenaline through his body and jump-started his heart. The first thing he noticed was that the television show was in color. He looked at his watch. Four-eighteen. Who the hell would bang on his door at four-eighteen in the morning?

The pounding quickened into the sound of desperation. Jack grabbed his cane, resting all his weight on the sturdy wood as he struggled to stand. The pain in his hip made him grimace, but he did it, taking a second to adjust his balance. "Hold on, dammit," he said, but not loud enough to be heard over the fist on wood.

He lurched to the table and picked up his weapon, his thumb resting on the safety. Then he made his way to the door. He looked through the peephole and saw the distorted face of a man, someone familiar, but he couldn't place him. He leaned on his good leg, resting the cane against his bad leg, and then opened the door.

"McCabe," the man said, his voice so high with tension he sounded like a woman. "Thank God!"

Jack's gaze moved down to the two bundles in the man's arms. One of them was a child, wrapped up in a quilt. The other was a stuffed pillowcase. He looked once more at his visitor and remembered where he'd seen him before. "Roy."

"Yeah, Roy. Roy Chandler. From downstairs. Listen, man," he said, edging his way inside, "I need your help."

"I'm on medical leave. You'll have to call the department."

"No, not that. I…it's my wife. She's hurt. Real bad. I need to get to the hospital."

"You want my car?" Jack asked, confused.

Roy held the kid out, pushing the bundle against Jack's chest. Jack grabbed hold with his free arm, instinctively, surprised at the weight. His cane fell, bouncing off the door frame. "What the hell?" he said, trying not to bounce off the door frame himself.

"I have to get to the hospital," Roy said, dropping the pillowcase by Jack's feet. "Now. I can't wait and I can't take her with me. I'll be back. An hour. Two at the most." Roy stepped back quickly, moving neatly out of range. He looked behind him, down toward the parking lot. Then he turned again to face Jack, the desperation that had made his voice so high now in his eyes. "I'll be back," he said. "Take care of her. She's all…" He didn't finish, just turned and darted toward the staircase.

"Hey!" Jack started forward, but realized instantly it was a mistake. The pain in his hip almost doubled him over, and it was all he could do not to drop the child. When he was finally able to stand again, Roy was halfway down to the parking lot.

Jack hobbled to the couch and used his free arm to balance himself. He swept last Thursday's *Chronicle* to the floor, then put the kid down, moving the quilt aside to make sure the small bundle was in fact a living, breathing child. It was. A girl. Maybe four or five. Blond hair a mess of curls, pale skin with pink lips. Amazingly enough, she was sound asleep. He wondered how she could do that.

He'd think about that later. For now, he had to try to catch Roy Chandler. He turned, and even that small motion had to be timed, weighed carefully, planned and executed with a deliberation that made Jack sure he'd found hell and moved in. A trickle of sweat itched at the back of his neck, but he couldn't walk and chew gum at the same time, let alone pick up his cane, hold his gun and rub his neck. His focus remained on the cane and he forced himself forward. Step by bloody step until he reached the door.

He put his gun in the waistband of his pants so he could grab hold of the door while he bent for his cane. He felt as if he were using someone else's body—an old man's, weak and brittle. The joke was, inside he still felt like the basketball player he'd been in college. The cop who'd aced the obstacle course at the academy. The man he'd been only four short months ago.

He straightened and shifted his weight to the cane. He looked back, but the kid hadn't moved. Then he went outside, the cold wet of the Houston night a jarring contrast to the cozy heat in his apartment.

Looking down over the balcony, he saw that Roy hadn't gotten into his car yet. He stood under the light from the pole behind him, staring at a car pulling into the lot. As Jack hobbled toward the stairs, he kept checking on Roy and then shifted his attention to the car. A Ford Taurus, dark, two men in the front. He relaxed, recognizing the unmarked police car. HPD had half a dozen just like it for the vice boys.

Knowing they'd check out Roy and hold him for a while, Jack slowed his pace, but didn't stop. As he reached the staircase, he realized he hadn't asked what hospital Roy's wife was in or what had happened to her. Why in hell he'd have to leave his kid behind, especially with him. Jack didn't know spit about kids, except that they were noisy and they usually smelled bad.

The steps weren't easy for him, and he had to lean on the railing just the right way. As he lowered his bad leg, he heard two short pops, and he froze, except for his thumb which released the safety on his gun almost of its own accord. The sound was unmistakable. Gunshots through a silencer.

He looked down to see Roy on the ground, a dark stain spreading on his chest. The cop in the passenger seat jumped out of the car and bent over to evaluate his work.

Jack's every instinct urged him to hurry. To find out what the hell was going on. This was bad. It was bad in a way he could feel all the way to his bones. Cops didn't shoot like that. Not an unarmed man.

But he couldn't hurry. The best he could do was take the steps one at a time, forcing the pain to the back of his mind to be remembered in vivid detail later. He watched the cop stand and head back for the car. "Hey! Wait!"

But either the cop didn't hear him or he didn't care, because he just kept on going. Even though Jack tried like hell, he couldn't make out the guy's features. The way he stood, he was more of a shadow than a man, and then he was back in the car. The driver hit the gas so hard the car lurched forward, tires squealing.

A light went on in the apartment on Jack's left, and then a woman's head poked out the door. She looked at him with terror in her eyes.

"Call 911," he said. "Now."

Her head snapped back and the door slammed shut, and he could hear the dead bolt click as he finally reached the parking lot. He hoped the woman would do as he asked, but from the way Roy looked, she didn't have to rush. Jack could see the unnatural attitude of the body, the crooked way Roy's head lay.

Cursing his luck, he made his way over, and as he moved next to Roy he saw the dark pool of blood blossom around the motionless arms and chest. A man's life seeping into the filthy asphalt.

Then he saw a movement. One he hadn't expected. Roy's head tilted to the left, and Jack saw his eyes open, then close. Jack bent his good leg, holding on to the cane with all his might as he eased down to his knees. It hurt like hell, but Roy was alive. Trying to say something.

"Protect her…" he said, his voice as whispery as a ghost. "Get the money. Don't…" He stopped, frozen in a seizure, then relaxing nearer to death. "The cops… Don't…"

The last word was drowned in a sickening gurgle, and Roy was gone. Jack put his hand to Roy's neck, checking the jugular for a pulse. Nothing. Stone-cold nothing.

Jack looked back at the apartment building. Several lights were on now, although no one had come outside. They all stayed behind their plywood doors, as if that could keep them safe. He heard a distant siren, which, he supposed, was all he had a right to expect.

If he hadn't been caught so off guard, he never would have let Roy leave his kid behind. He'd never have let Roy leave at all, at least not until he understood what was going on. But he had been caught, and he had taken the kid and let the father go. So while everyone else in the building stayed inside, peeking through parted curtains, he was left with a kid, a body and one hell of a question. Why had the cops gunned down Roy Chandler in cold blood?

It took him a couple of awkward minutes to stand again. By that time, a patrol car, familiar blue, arrived. The car stopped a couple of hundred feet away, so the cops wouldn't contaminate the crime scene. The doors opened and Jack recognized Bill Haggart immediately, just from the way the man stood.

Haggart was an old-timer who'd never managed to pass the sergeant's exam. He'd gotten Jack out of a scrape or two through the years, and while Jack didn't consider him the brightest bulb in the chandelier, he was a good cop who understood the street.

"Bored, were you?" Haggart said as he gave Roy's body a once-over.

"Yeah," Jack said, wishing like hell he could sit down. "Finished all my crossword puzzles."

Jack didn't know the driver of the patrol car well. Fetzer was his name. Paul Fetzer. Young guy, Nordic-looking with his white-blond hair and pale skin. Jack had heard he was a hot dog, looking to get into homicide, but just like everyone else, he needed to do his time. Putting him with Haggart was probably good for both of them.

"What happened?" Paul asked, moving next to Haggart. "You know him?"

"He lives in the building," Jack said. "I've seen him around."

"You see who did this?" Haggart asked, his voice dramatically sharper now that Paul was listening.

Jack decided right then that he wasn't going to tell them about the unmarked car. He wasn't sure why, just a feeling. He'd learned to listen to his gut reactions. At least most of the time. The bullet in his hip was a good reminder of what happened when he didn't. "I saw a car. It was too dark to make out anything much. It was a sedan, late model. They used a silencer. I heard two shots."

"They?" Paul repeated. "There was more than one?"

Jack nodded. "Driver and passenger. Both males. I couldn't see if they were Caucasians. The light hit the car wrong, and all I got were shadows. I couldn't run after them to get the license plate."

"Pardon me for being blunt," Haggart said, "but you look like shit."

"Thanks."

"I mean it. The ambulance should be here any second. Maybe you should let the paramedics take a look at you."

"I'm fine. You might as well call them off. Get someone from the medical examiner's office down here."

"Did you touch anything?" Paul asked as he moved closer to Roy and crouched down. He pulled out his flashlight, and focused the beam on Roy's chest. It looked to Jack like it had been a large-caliber weapon. There was a hell of a lot of damage.

"I touched his neck for a pulse," Jack said. "That's it."

"How'd you happen to see this?" Haggart asked.

"Insomnia," Jack answered, not lying exactly. Just not telling the whole story.

"Out for a walk at this time of night?"

He shook his head. "I heard something. I came outside, saw the car, heard the shots. By the time I made it down the stairs, Roy here was dead and the car was long gone."

"Roy what?"

"Chandler. I think he lived on the second floor. Around back."

The ambulance came screaming into the parking lot, but the driver cut the siren immediately, filling the night with an echo of sadness. Jack shifted a bit, which was a mistake. He winced and sucked in a sharp breath.

Haggart moved closer to him, probably worried that he was goning to fall on his face. "Why don't you go on up," he said, his voice concerned. "We can take care of things down here. We know where to find you tomorrow."

Jack didn't take long to decide. He needed to sit down. Take a pill. Make sure the kid upstairs hadn't fallen off the couch. "Yeah," he said. "I'll be around."

A female paramedic Jack didn't know circled the police car and knelt beside Roy. She put her kit next to her knee and gestured to Paul to back off. The young cop did as she asked, but he didn't seem real happy to be brushed aside.

Jack didn't give a damn. He had his own problems. He nodded to Haggart, then started the long voyage home. Walking across the parking lot was hard enough. The stairs were going to be murder.

THE KID WAS STILL SLEEPING when he got back. After three pain pills and about half an hour of sitting still on the lounger, Jack was able to stand again. He crossed to the girl, noticing for the first time that she had a doll clutched in her right hand. It wasn't a very nice doll. The hair was all ratty, with big holes in the scalp where the strands had been tied. One eye was open, the other closed in a perpetual wink. There was a stain on the doll's cheek that looked like blue ink.

What a damn mess. He didn't like dirty cops, and he didn't like cryptic deathbed messages, and he didn't like the fact that the sun was going to rise any minute and he hadn't slept. The kid was going to wake up eventually, and she'd want to know where her parents were, and she'd cry and carry on and…oh, hell. Jack made it back to the lounger and sank gratefully onto the cushion. The smart thing to do was call family services as soon as possible. Go to the captain and tell him what he heard and what he saw. End this thing before it went any further.

Even if there was a crime to be solved, he wasn't the man to solve it. Not anymore. Not with this body. All he was good for was watching daytime television.

HE WOKE UP to a pair of blue eyes. Big round blue eyes, inches from his face. The kid was up and she'd climbed onto his lap, somehow avoiding his bad hip.

One inch to the right, and he'd have been one sorry ex-cop.

"Where's my daddy?"

The girl had her doll under one arm and her quilt under the other. She looked amazingly calm, as if she woke up in a stranger's house all the time.

"I have to go potty."

Perfect. She had to go potty. He had no idea what that entailed—well, except for the fundamentals, of course. Was he supposed to help her? Lead her to the bathroom and leave? Change her diaper?

She wasn't wearing a diaper. He could see that from the way her Little Mermaid pajamas fit. "Climb down," he said. "Carefully."

She obeyed him, moving slowly and cautiously until she stood next to the chair, but she never took her eyes off him, not even for a second.

"Can you do it by yourself?"

"What?"

"Can you go potty by yourself?"

She nodded, the curls on her head waving with the movement.

Jack pointed to the hallway. "It's right over there," he said. "Just walk down the hall."

She blinked at him, then turned, her quilt trailing behind her as she padded toward the bathroom. He focused on his own problem: getting up and making coffee. He swallowed another pill, then went to the kitchen for a water chaser. His leg felt stiffer than usual, but he expected that. The doctors had said the pain would be temporary, lasting just a few months.

In his opinion, four was more than a few. So when was this miraculous recovery supposed to kick in?

At least he'd gotten his morning routine worked out. He'd set up the kitchen to require the fewest steps necessary. Coffee, filters, the machine, all next to the sink. After he finished pouring and counting, he checked his watch. Seven-thirty. He'd call family services at eight.

He heard a shuffle and looked in the living room. The girl stood by the hallway, staring at him. "Where's my daddy?" she asked again.

He didn't know what to say. How to say it. The kid was so young.

She blinked a few times, as if she was trying to get him into focus. "I want Hailey," she said.

Hailey. Who the hell was— "You mean that woman down the hall? The blond lady?"

The girl nodded. "Hailey. She's my baby-sitter."

"Hailey," he repeated, thinking about where he'd seen her. In the laundry room, that was it. A couple of months ago. With the kid. She'd helped him carry his clothes upstairs. "Let's go see Hailey, okay?"

The kid nodded. "Is my daddy there?"

"We'll see," he said, chickening out. He started toward her, and she went to the door. She put her doll on the floor and grasped the doorknob. It took her a few tries, but she got the door open, and then she picked up her doll again. She didn't say anything. She didn't look scared. She waited patiently for him to reach her side and then closed the door behind them.

Something wasn't right. He didn't know much

about kids, but even he knew she ought to be scared out of her wits.

She led him down the walkway, past the five doors that separated his place from Hailey's. Then she stopped. Shifted her doll under her arm and put her thumb in her mouth.

Jack knocked on Hailey's door. Checked the kid, then knocked again, praying the woman was home. Then he heard the dead bolt slip and the door swung open.

She was still in her bathrobe. She looked at him with a question in her eyes, then she saw the girl. "Megan!"

"Is my daddy here?"

Hailey's gaze moved back to Jack. "What's going on?"

"Can we talk?"

Her brow furrowed with concern, but she didn't press him. She picked Megan up, then held the door open for him. The second he walked inside, he knew he'd done the right thing. The kid would feel safe here. Hell, *he* felt safe here. And he hadn't felt safe in about a hundred years.

Chapter Two

Hailey Bishop closed the door and turned to her guest. She recognized him, although she didn't remember his name. John or Jack or something like that. She also knew he was a police officer, although she'd never seen him in a uniform.

He stood in the middle of her living room, leaning on his cane, favoring his left leg. She wondered if he'd been hurt on the job, but then Megan tightened her grip on her throat and Hailey forgot about the policeman's problems. "What happened?" she asked him as she rubbed Megan's back to calm her down.

He shook his head, and she realized he didn't want to speak in front of the child. She didn't like this. Her stomach clenched and the hairs on the back of her neck bristled. Even so, she smiled as she walked near the television and lowered Megan to the floor. Gently she took the girl's quilt out of her hand and spread it on the carpet. "What kind of juice do you want?"

Megan thought a moment. "Apple."

"Apple it is." Hailey turned on the television,

changing the channel until she found cartoons. Then she went to the kitchen and got one of the juice boxes she kept on hand. By the time she got back, the little girl was sitting cross-legged, her doll tucked safely into her lap. When Hailey handed her the juice, the girl smiled, then went back to watching Tom and Jerry.

Hailey turned to the policeman. He really didn't look good. Aside from his obvious discomfort, his cheeks seemed hollow and his skin pale. He hadn't shaved for a while and his dark stubble made him look gruff and hard. But his eyes told her something different. His gaze was on Megan, and the way he looked at her said worlds about the man. The little one was in some kind of trouble and he knew it. More than that, he was concerned about her.

As she signaled him to join her in the kitchen, she looked beyond the stubble and the brooding eyes. She'd thought he was handsome the first time she'd seen him, and that hadn't changed. She wanted to know what had happened to him, whether someone was taking care of him. But that was for later.

He made it to her dining room and sat down heavily in the first chair he came to. He took a deep breath and let it out slowly. Standing must hurt.

"Coffee?" she asked.

He nodded. "That would be great."

"How do you like it?"

"Black," he said, watching her keenly as she went into the kitchen. "I'm Jack McCabe," he said. "I've seen you around."

"Yes, I recognized you, too. I didn't know you knew Roy and Megan."

"I don't. I mean, I've seen him a few times, said hello, but that's all."

She poured the coffee into two mugs and brought them to the table. He took his with a grateful but worried smile. "So what happened?" she asked.

"Did you hear the sirens this morning?"

She nodded. "I didn't realize they were at the complex. I'm so used to hearing them these days."

"They were here, all right. Roy," he said, lowering his voice to a whisper, "was killed this morning."

Hailey almost dropped her mug. She put it down on the table as she fought for breath. "Killed? Are you sure?"

Jack nodded. "I'm sure."

"How?" she asked too loudly. Moving closer to Jack, she asked again, "How?"

"He was shot."

"What? Were you there? Was Megan there?"

He shook his head. "Megan was safe. She didn't see a thing. It wasn't a random shooting. Whoever killed him did it on purpose."

"Oh, my God," Hailey said, more to herself than to Jack. She couldn't quite wrap her head around this horrific piece of news. Roy, dead? It was too absurd to be true. "How did you get Megan?"

"I didn't have much choice. Roy came to my door this morning. He shoved her at me, then ran off. He said he had to go to the hospital. That his wife was sick."

"Wife? He's not married. His wife died several years ago."

Jack looked over at Megan, sitting so quietly. Somehow he wasn't surprised that Roy had lied. "Does she have any other family?"

"I think so. But not here in Houston. There might be an aunt in Florida. What did the police say?"

"Not much. But I'm gonna go to the station this morning and find out all I can."

"You want me to watch her?"

He nodded. "Until I can get social services out here."

The thought of Megan being surrounded by strangers, even well-meaning strangers, was unbearable. "No, please," Hailey said. "Don't call them. I'll watch her."

"That's fine for today, but at some point…"

"Let's deal with that later. After Megan has some time to get used to…" She sighed. "Poor little thing."

"Yeah," he said. "It stinks."

"Do you have any of her things? Her clothes?"

"There's a pillowcase stuffed with her things back at my place. I haven't looked in it."

"What do you say we do that now? I want to get her dressed, and then I'll fix her some breakfast."

"You don't have to go to work?"

She shook her head. "I work here, out of my apartment. I design web sites."

Jack looked at her again, more carefully this time. She was sort of attractive, but that wasn't what drew him to her. There was a calmness about her, a serenity, that he'd never felt from another person before. No wonder Megan had wanted to come here.

"What's wrong?" she asked.

He shook his head. "We'd better go."

She gave him a questioning look, one that forced him to focus on her eyes. Blue, very blue. And kind. He could see where a man would go for a woman like her.

"I'll go dress and be right back," she said. "There's more coffee if you want it."

He nodded as she headed for her bedroom. When she was gone, his gaze moved to the girl. She seemed calm. But what did he know?

As he waited for Hailey to return, he tapped his fingers on the tabletop, thinking about this morning. About the Taurus. Maybe it hadn't been an HPD vehicle. It was dark. He wasn't exactly at his mental peak. It certainly didn't make sense. He knew most of the cops, at least from downtown. No one he knew would have done something so blatantly illegal. So if it wasn't cops, then who? Roy had known someone was after him.

Hailey came back, dressed in worn blue jeans and a pale blue sweater that buttoned down the front. The outfit showed off her curves very nicely. She went straight to Megan. "What do you say we go get dressed?"

Megan looked up. "It's bath time after *Sesame Street.*"

"I see," Hailey said. "Perhaps Mr. McCabe will let us use his bathtub."

Megan looked at him briefly, then back to Hailey. "I want to go home."

Hailey picked the girl up. "Gosh, you're getting so big!" she said. "Pretty soon, you'll be taller than this whole building!"

Megan giggled.

"We can't go home, sweet pea," Hailey said, her voice as soft as a feather pillow. "Not just yet."

Megan didn't respond. She simply laid her head on Hailey's shoulder.

Jack stood up, glad he'd taken that extra pain pill. His hip hurt, but not too badly. As Hailey walked to the door, he headed for the quilt and the doll, still on the floor in front of the television.

"Oh, wait," she said, guessing what he was about to do. "I'll get those."

"I can do it." A quick flash of anger seared his insides. "Just take care of the kid."

"Sorry."

He hadn't meant to be so gruff with her. But dammit, he wasn't totally helpless. To show her, he leaned over his cane neatly and came up again with Megan's things.

"That didn't hurt?" she asked.

He shrugged. "It's not so bad."

She sighed as she turned to the door. "It must be hard to be so macho all the time."

He grinned. "Later, if you're nice, I'll crush a beer can on my forehead for you."

"I don't know if my girlish heart could take it."

He made his way slowly out the door, grateful the

woman had a sense of humor. He had the feeling she'd need it.

HAILEY PUT MEGAN DOWN beside Jack's recliner. The room was so dark it was hard to believe it was daytime. It reminded her of a bear's cave, albeit one with a large-screen television set as a centerpiece. There wasn't a picture on the wall or even a plant. Old newspapers were piled up beside the couch, and empty beer bottles, three of them, sat on the small table by his chair. The place needed a good cleaning and a lot more light.

"There's the pillowcase," he said, pointing to the end of the couch. "I guess you can take her back to your place, huh?"

She smiled at him, making a decision that second. "If you don't mind, I'd like to bathe her here."

Jack looked at her as if she was nuts. "Why?"

"I'd just feel better waiting with her here. Until you get back."

He shrugged. "Suit yourself. The bathtub is pretty clean. There are towels in the cupboard. He turned and walked down the hall to his bedroom.

His apartment was identical to hers, at least architecturally. But where hers was a warm nest, his was a place to hide from the world. She wondered again how he'd been hurt. And how awful it must be for a man as virile as him to be trapped in a broken body.

She noticed a book peeking out from underneath the TV guide, and her curiosity got the better of her. She lifted the guide and saw that it was a paperback edition of *The Sun Also Rises* by Ernest Hemingway. Interesting.

Jack came back a second after she stopped snooping. He'd changed into a plain white business shirt, open at the collar, but he still wore his jeans. He also had on a leather jacket, and with his somehow dangerous face and those deep brown eyes, she felt a shock of physical awareness hit her where it counted.

"Here," he said. He held out a piece of paper to her. She took it but she didn't look at it. She was too busy wondering about her reaction to him. He wasn't her usual type. She liked kind men, calm men. Men who called their mothers on Sunday nights.

"My pager number," he said. "Just in case."

All her wayward thoughts vanished in the blink of an eye as she was brought back to the moment by a dose of cold reality. There was a killer loose. A murderer. "You don't think…"

"Just in case you need me to bring home some milk or something."

"Right," she said, not believing him. She took Megan's hand in hers, while Jack adjusted his jacket, and it was then she caught sight of his gun, neatly holstered against his rib cage. It shook her to realize it was a real gun, capable of killing, meant to kill. She'd never been this close to a gun before.

"Are you going to tell her?" he asked, lowering his voice, even though Megan was right there.

She squeezed Megan's hand gently. "Yes. Now go on. Find out what you can. We'll be here when you get back."

He looked at them one more time, then made his

way to the door. She wondered how he was going to drive, but it didn't seem prudent to bring that up. Instead, she led Megan down the hall to the bathroom, listening for the sound of the door shutting and his key in the lock. She heard both, and she breathed a little easier. Although she didn't think she would relax completely until this whole thing got straightened out.

Who would want to kill Roy Chandler? He'd always seemed like such a nice man. He paid her generously for baby-sitting. He certainly loved Megan. Perhaps Jack was wrong, and it was just one of those horrible mistakes, a drive-by shooting or something.

It didn't matter really, not to the little one. Either way, her father was dead. She had no one now. Not even an aunt in Florida. Hailey hadn't liked lying to Jack, but there was no way she would let social services take this child away.

Megan put her doll on the sink counter, then pulled off her pajama top. That spurred Hailey to start the water running in the tub. She got down on her knees and tested the temperature until she got it right.

She had to admit the bathroom was cleaner than she'd imagined. Except for the *Sports Illustrated* swimsuit edition on the floor, it was very nicely put together. Clean towels, a sparkling sink, and the tub was spick-and-span.

Megan had finished undressing, and now she stood next to Hailey, waiting. Leaning slightly against her.

Just touching. But, bless her heart, she appeared quite stoic and ready to get down to business.

Hailey put her in the tub, and for the first few minutes they both concentrated on washing Megan. The soap wasn't Hailey's usual brand, but Megan liked the scent. The bath was a quiet affair, which was unsettling. The girl loved taking baths and usually she talked Hailey's ear off. Not today. She finished quickly, not dawdling to play. She stood up in the tub, her body shiny and innocent, her eyes wide with muted fear. "Are we going to see my daddy now?"

Hailey couldn't put it off any longer. But, oh, how she wished she didn't have to shatter this little bunny. She got the big blue towel from the rack, then reached for Megan and lifted her out of the tub. Quickly, before Megan could get a chill, she wrapped the towel around her. Hailey rubbed her legs and arms to make her dry and warm, and then she put her arms around her. "Sweet pea," she began, making sure her voice was as tender and safe as she could muster, "Daddy…" She swallowed. Took a deep breath. "Daddy had to leave, sweetheart."

"Where?"

"Daddy went to heaven, Megan. He went to see your mommy."

Megan didn't say anything. But Hailey could feel her little body tremble.

"He loves you very much," she whispered. "And he hated to leave you. If he could have stayed, he would have."

"Can't I go, too?"

Hailey closed her eyes and felt the sting of tears. "Not yet, baby."

Megan's chin quivered, and she began to cry, her tears too big for such a little girl. Sobs that tore Hailey's heart in two, made her want to scream at the God who could do this to such a dear child.

Megan buried her head in Hailey's shoulder, and they sat like that for a long time. The mournful sounds of too much pain echoing off the tiled walls, filling the world with sadness. Hailey rocked her back and forth, letting her be, letting her weep until her tears stopped of their own accord. Until she sighed with resignation. It wasn't over. Megan's grief would go on for a lifetime, but for now, she'd worn herself out, which was a blessing.

Megan sniffed, then sat up so she was looking into Hailey's eyes. "Can I stay with you?" she asked, her voice so tiny it almost wasn't there.

Hailey nodded. "Of course, honey. Don't worry. I won't let you go."

JACK GOT OUT OF HIS TRUCK and leaned against the door for a while. It was cold for Houston. Cold but still humid, which made the frigid air seep right into his bones. Right into his wound.

Driving hadn't helped. He probably shouldn't have done it, but then he probably shouldn't have become a cop in the first place. But now that he was, he had a job to do. At least, as much of a job as his damn hip would allow. He still didn't want to say anything about the unmarked police car. Not until he had more facts. Accusing his brethren of murder wasn't something to do lightly. There had to be another explanation.

He pushed himself off the car and walked through the underground parking lot toward the elevator. The sound of a revving engine echoed off the concrete walls. He thought about what was happening in his apartment as he waited for the elevator to come. It was right, to have Hailey talk to the girl. They knew each other. They cared about each other. He would have been in the way.

The doors opened, and he walked into the small cab, pressing the button for the first floor. As the elevator rose, he reached for his wallet and pulled out his ID, clipping it to his shirt pocket. It was a move he'd done so many times he rarely even thought about it. He did now. This ID was more than a way to get upstairs. It was, like his badge, who he was. Homicide detective. Twelve-year veteran. One mean son of a bitch. A single bullet had stripped him of his way of life. One goddamn bullet.

The doors opened and he walked into the warm air of the downtown station. Jenny Cole sat behind the desk. When she saw him she smiled, and her eyes went right to the cane.

"Jenny," he said, walking as quickly and evenly as he could.

"Hi, Jack. How are you?"

"Fine, thanks." He handed her his gun as he went through the metal detector and then she handed it back.

"We've missed you. And worried about you."

"Thanks, but I'm pretty involved with my new football career. Quarterbacking is hell."

She smiled, but it didn't reach her eyes. They were too filled with pity to let anything else in.

He holstered his weapon and crossed to the central elevator. He didn't look back at her, although he could feel her gaze.

When he got to the fourth floor, he stepped out, hoping no one was in the hall. He got his wish. It was quiet, and he looked at the big bulletproof glass doors that separated the two worlds. Inside, a universe of cops, neat, organized, with their own code of living and of dying. Outside, the other universe, most of it messy and complicated. He didn't belong on this side. And he didn't belong on the other.

He took a step forward, horribly aware of the pain and the feel of the cane in his hand, and of dragging his bad leg and leaning his weight on the other. He felt like a marionette with cut strings. Awkward. Useless.

But at least he could still use a computer. He could use his brain. Maybe it would be enough.

Although he doubted it.

Chapter Three

Hailey sat on the edge of the couch, her gaze fixed on the sleeping child.

It was nearly noon, and Megan had been asleep for almost two hours. The poor kid had exhausted herself. At least she'd gotten some comfort from her quilt and her doll. The three of them were on the floor, just like naptime at Hailey's. Last Christmas she'd bought Megan a brand-new doll, a beautiful one with a full head of hair and not a single felt-pen mark on her body. But Megan was a loyal little thing. She'd thanked Hailey, then gone right back to lugging Tottie around.

Hailey tried to remember if she'd had a favorite doll. One she couldn't be parted from. But it wasn't the day for her own memories.

She forced herself to look up, to see where she was. Jack's television, dark and silent, reminded her of the statues on Easter Island. The icon of worship for people who didn't get out much. Which didn't fit into the admittedly sketchy picture she had of Jack.

Grace had told her he was single. And that an assortment of women dropped by at all hours. Grace also said she'd seen him in his skivvies once, by accident, and that pound for pound he was the best-looking man she'd seen since Elvis.

But then, Grace also believed aliens took all the good parking spots at Luby's.

Hailey had wondered how Grace had seen him in his underwear. The woman was sixty if she was a day, and she chain-smoked unfiltered Camels, which had stained her teeth an interesting shade of brown.

When had they had that discussion? Oh, yes. It was last Easter. When Hailey had brought her downstairs neighbor a cooked ham. Last Easter, Jack had been fine. It was only two months ago that Hailey had seen him in the laundry room. Seen him using the cane. She'd been with Megan that day. And she remembered thinking then that despite Jack's brusque manners, he was a devilishly handsome rogue.

She smiled. Rogue. She'd been reading too many historical romances.

Even if he didn't fit the rogue category, there was something about him... She got up, filled with nervous energy. She went to his kitchen and saw a few dirty plates in the sink, a few clean ones in the plastic drainer on the counter. Discarded coffee filters and beer cans were all she could make out in his trash. She opened his refrigerator and sighed. Not much there. Mustard. Beer. A loaf of bread and a big salami. He'd never heal with this kind of diet.

Wondering how he'd managed so far, she went to the sink and turned on the water. There were no gloves, but there was detergent and a sponge. Having something to do helped. It made her calmer. It gave her time to strategize. When Jack came home, he was going to want to call social services, and there was no question in her mind that she wasn't going to let him. The idea of Megan going to a stranger after all she'd been through made her sick to her stomach. No matter what, Megan was going to stay.

After finishing the dishes, she cleaned the counters and the coffeemaker. Picked up the old newspapers and tied them with some cord she found under the sink. Then she dusted a bit and, with nothing left to do, headed down the hall to Jack's bedroom.

His decor was consistent, if nothing else. Only the bare necessities. A bed, no headboard. A dresser. A chair. Not even a chair. She shook her head, not surprised that the bed was unmade. Given his condition, she had to wonder when he'd last changed the sheets. It would be a difficult task with a cane.

Was it too personal a thing to do? She didn't know the man at all, and now she wanted to change his sheets? Her own need for a purpose silenced her doubts, and she went to the hall closet to get fresh ones.

He only had two other sets. Both beige. Utilitarian. Fine for a man whose life was filled with work and friends, but awful for a man who was virtually housebound.

She checked on Megan, who was still sound asleep and clutching her doll, and then headed back to his room. It took no time at all to strip the bed. When it

was bare, she hurried, because the room felt too
much like a prison cell.

Once she was done, she dusted in there, too, wishing she could vacuum the place. It wasn't as if she
was a neat freak or anything, but Jack had done a
good deed for Megan. He'd brought Megan to her.
It was only right that Hailey do something nice for
him in return.

Then she remembered the pillowcase. She'd barely
looked in it when she'd pulled out Megan's fresh
clothes. Hailey hurried back down the hall, and just
as she took hold of the pillowcase, she heard his key
in the lock.

She felt her stomach tighten as she turned. Jack
walked in slowly. He looked exhausted. His gaze
went to Megan, asleep on her quilt on the floor, and
Hailey saw his shoulders relax. Then he spotted her,
standing by the couch. "I haven't gone through it
yet," she said, holding out the pillowcase. "I just
got her clothes out after her bath."

He nodded, locked the dead bolt, then took off his
jacket. After leaning slightly against the door, he
rolled up his sleeves past his elbows. His arms were
lightly dusted with dark hair. She could clearly see
the road map of tendons and muscle on his forearms.
Very masculine. He winced as he pushed off toward
the kitchen, and she fought the urge to offer to help
him. He wasn't one of the children she tended, and
besides, she remembered his angry reaction the first
time. Still, it hurt, somehow, to watch him move
across the room, leaning so heavily on his cane.

"What's this?" he asked when he turned the kitchen light on.

"I hope you don't mind. I couldn't sit still."

He grunted a noncommittal response, then poured himself a glass of water. She approached him as he drank, fascinated by his Adam's apple, at the size of his thirst. When he finished, he wiped his arm across his mouth, his gaze on hers as if he'd known she'd been watching him. "Did you tell her?" he asked, keeping his deep voice low.

She nodded. "She was very brave. But it hasn't really hit her yet. It's going to take a long while for her to adjust to this. To accept that her father isn't coming back."

Jack moved to the kitchen table and sat heavily in a chair. His cane clattered loudly to the linoleum floor, but he didn't even give it a glance. "Not only is he not coming back," he said, "he wasn't really here."

"What?" She pulled out the chair opposite him and sat down, laying the pillowcase between them.

"Roy Chandler wasn't his name."

"Seriously?"

He answered her with a look that said he was dead serious.

"Who was he?"

"A charmer named Barry Strangis. From Oklahoma. Incarcerated twice for armed robbery, once in 1972 and again in 1980."

"Oh, man."

"Yeah," he said. His gaze moved to something behind her, and at first she thought Megan had gotten up, but when she turned, she saw she was still sound asleep. He had looked at his chair in the living room. Looked at it with need.

She stood up, went to his television table and got his bottle of pain pills. After she put the bottle on the kitchen table, she took his glass and filled it once more with water. She handed it to him as she sat down again.

He didn't seem pleased. His eyebrows furrowed and his lips pressed together tightly. Finally he said, "What are you doing?"

"Getting your pills. Water."

"I know that, but why?"

"Because it's time for you to take a pill."

"How do you know?"

"From the look on your face. You seemed... pained."

"I always look like this."

She smiled, then tried to hide it.

"What's so funny?" he asked, his voice even rougher than before.

"I've always admired a good curmudgeon," she said. "George Bernard Shaw. Scrooge. They lend balance to the world."

"Are you making fun of me?"

She nodded. "Yes, I am."

"Well, knock it off."

"Then take your pill."

He glared at her for another long moment, but then he opened the bottle, shook a pill onto his palm and popped it into his mouth. He drank the entire glass of water, and once more, he wiped his mouth with his arm.

The movement should have been gauche, but it wasn't. He reminded her of Marlon Brando in *Streetcar*. Rough and cruel, but only because it hid a vulnerability so deep he didn't know where to turn.

"So what's in the case?" he asked.

She shifted her attention to the pillowcase, dumping the contents on the table. The first thing she saw was a picture frame. She moved to pick it up at the same time he did, and their fingers brushed. The contact surprised her, and she jerked her hand back. He grew very still for a moment, then lifted the frame so he could see the picture. "Hmm," he said.

"What?"

He turned it around.

"That's Megan's mother," Hailey said. "Patricia."

Jack looked at it again. "She was pretty."

"Megan looks a lot like her. She'll be a beautiful woman."

"Do you know when this Patricia died?"

Hailey shook her head. "Not really. But I think it was after they moved here. I started working for Roy two years ago."

"What's that?" He pointed to a sheet of paper inside a plastic bag.

Hailey turned it over to find a recipe. For mulligatawny stew. Handwritten, stained. She passed it to Jack.

"Why would he give her this?"

"I don't know. Maybe it's all he has in his wife's handwriting."

Jack shook his head, then put the recipe aside. He picked up a bank passbook and opened it. "Four hundred and fifty dollars. In the name of Megan Chandler."

"When was the last deposit?"

"At Christmas."

She didn't see much else of interest. Just clothes, which she proceeded to fold. There were jeans and sweatshirts, a few dresses, a jacket. Two pairs of shoes, a stack of panties and three sets of pajamas.

"He knew he was going to be gone awhile," Jack said. "Or that he might never come back."

"It appears so. But there's something I've been wondering all morning. Why did he bring Megan to you, when I was just down the hall?"

Jack's frown deepened. "The only reason I can think of is that he knew I was a cop."

"So he must have guessed he was in trouble. Bad trouble."

"Given the fact that he's a corpse now, he guessed right."

"And he didn't say anything else?"

He looked at her, studying her closely. She thought he was going to say something, but then he just shook his head. She had the feeling he wasn't telling her everything. Maybe that was for the best. She didn't want to know anything that would get her into trouble. Not when she had to look out for Megan.

As if he'd sensed her protective thought, he nodded toward the living room. "We should call."

Hailey caught his gaze and held it. "No, we're not going to call."

"We're not?"

"No," she repeated. "I want her here."

"You can't do that."

"Maybe not. But I'm going to all the same."

He leaned back in his chair, giving her a repeat of his unhappy face. It made him look dangerous in a way. Not spooky dangerous. Sexy dangerous.

"I promised her that she could stay with me," she said. "She has no one else. And she's too vulnerable to be taken away by strangers. It would make things infinitely worse."

"The cops will find out he had a kid."

"I don't see that as an obstacle. I'm sure there are ways we could make them think Megan was away. I could tell Grace and a few other tenants. They'd help."

He closed his eyes for a moment, and when he looked back at her, he'd eased up on the frown. "For now," he said.

"Fair enough."

"But when things settle down…"

"We'll talk about it again."

"You design web sites? You should have been a lawyer."

"Thank you."

He leaned forward again, and she prepared for his retort, but instead, he frowned once more and nodded toward the living room. "Look who's awake."

Hailey turned to see Megan sitting up, clutching Tottie and sucking her thumb. "Hey, sweet pea," she said as she left Jack and his scowl. "You slept a long time."

Megan looked at her. "I want to go home," she said.

"I know you do, honey. But I'm afraid we can't go home just yet. Mr. McCabe and I are going to look after you, remember?"

She nodded slowly. Hailey thought she might start crying again, but she didn't. "Tottie's hungry," was all she said.

"I'll bet she is. And I'll bet you are, too. Tell you what. You stay here with Mr. McCabe, and I'll get us all lunch from my apartment and bring it back."

"I want to go, too."

"I'll only be gone a few minutes. Why don't you show Mr. McCabe your special blanket?"

Megan nodded, and Hailey wasn't sure it was a good thing. The girl was a scrapper. Always had been. She sometimes had a tendency to throw a dramatic tantrum when she didn't get her way, although the episodes were short-lived. To see her acquiesce so soon, and so stoically, told Hailey a lot. This little one was going to need a great deal of attention and a great deal of understanding.

"I'll be back," she said, turning to Jack. "I'll bring some food."

"I'll help," he said, leaning down to retrieve his cane.

"No, that's okay. You need to be here with Megan." Before he could argue, Hailey unlocked the apartment door and went outside. It was still chilly. She would put on a jacket before she returned.

As she walked toward her apartment, she felt nervous, as if someone was watching her. When she looked at the parking lot below, no one seemed to be there, although there were several unfamiliar cars in the lot. She shook the feeling off as understandable paranoia, but she walked faster and didn't feel better until she was inside her place. She bolted the door behind her. The feeling didn't completely disappear, and she understood right then that her own personal bubble of invulnerability had been shattered this morning. She wondered it she'd ever get it back again.

"THIS IS GARFIELD and he's the dog. And these are the bees, the mommy and daddy and baby, see?"

Jack nodded, feeling awkward and inept as he listened to Megan talk about her blanket. She continued to point out all the significant pictures—the little girl who was all alone, the eyes, the letters and numbers and the great big heart. It didn't make a whole lot of sense to him, but then he couldn't remember ever thinking about a quilt before. Megan certainly took it seriously, though. After each explanation, she waited for his nod and only then moved to the next.

So he kept nodding when there was a pause, but he wasn't thinking about the big bus or the bumblebee family. His thoughts were on the girl and her situation. She was an orphan, and even though Hailey wanted to keep her, the state still had control over her future. Unfortunately the state was a notoriously bad parent.

It would probably be better for the kid to stick with

Hailey, but if she did that and a relative showed up, there'd be big trouble. Who knows how attached Megan would become to Hailey? Then she'd have lost her parents and her guardian, and that wouldn't be something she could easily recover from. He'd seen that too many times to have any doubts. Kids taken from bad families, put into foster homes, then shuffled to another and another. Those kids didn't, as a rule, fare well. They ended up coming back home, only by then the parent state was usually in the form of a penitentiary.

At least she was a girl. Girls generally adjusted better than boys.

"...daddy?"

He heard the word and realized she'd asked him something. "What?"

"Do you know my daddy?"

Shoot. He'd hoped to avoid this. What was he supposed to say? Where the hell was Hailey? "Uh, yeah," he said. "Sure."

"Hailey says he went to heaven to see my mommy."

Dammit, where was she? How long could getting some food take? "Yeah, uh, well... Hailey's pretty smart."

"Does she baby-sit you, too?"

He smiled. "Not exactly."

"Oh." She frowned. "People don't come back from heaven."

He probably needed to say something else. Something reassuring. She looked up at him with those big blue eyes, just staring. Waiting. But he didn't have a clue. She might as well have been one of those bumblebees on the quilt for all he knew how to talk to her. He'd never been around kids, not like Megan, at least. He'd know what to say if she'd just tagged a building or sold drugs on the schoolyard. But this? He was way out of his league.

He blinked, but she didn't. She didn't move. "You want to watch some television?" he asked desperately.

She nodded, but did he detect a note of disappointment in her eyes? Had he already failed?

"I like *Reading Rainbow*," she said in a small voice. "And sometimes I watch *Barney*."

"Barney," he repeated, wishing he knew what she was talking about. "Sure you don't like to watch football?"

She shrugged.

"It's fun, trust me," he said, turning toward the television. The remote was on the TV table, and he switched on the set, grateful for the distraction. He clicked until he hit the Dolphins' game. Then he went to his chair and sank into it, grateful to be off his feet.

Megan came up next to him. "I've seen this game before at my house."

"Yeah? Well, good. Greatest game ever invented."

"My daddy says football is for jerks. He says the quarterboy doesn't know shit from shinola."

Jack jerked his gaze to Megan. "Pardon me?"

She sighed. "He says football is for jerks—"

"Yeah, yeah, I heard you. Maybe we'll look for this *Barney* show, after all."

"Okay," she said.

He flipped the channel and the next and the next until finally he found some cartoons. It wasn't *Barney,* but it wasn't football, either.

She moved closer to him, then before he could do a thing, she climbed into his lap and settled back. She adjusted her doll under her arm and put her thumb in her mouth.

It was the damndest thing.

Chapter Four

Jack gripped the arms of his chair, not sure what to do. He sent out a mental SOS for Hailey, but to no avail. Megan, on the other hand, seemed completely relaxed. She curved to his body, leaning her head on his upper arm, letting her legs dangle on each side of his. He said a quick thanks to whatever had made her pick his good side to climb on.

As it was, he wanted nothing more than to put her back on the floor where she belonged. But that would probably freak her out.

He went through another list of options, each one worse than the last. He couldn't jump up, that was for sure. He couldn't even talk his way out of this, because she was hardly more than a baby, for crying out loud.

He watched a cartoon mouse hit a cartoon cat with a frying pan, but he had no idea what had provoked the attack, because he was too busy thinking about the scent he'd just noticed. Not like perfume. Not even like a woman after a bath. This was a whole different smell. A vulnerable smell. He'd never been with a kid who didn't smell bad. Or who was so quiet. Except for the rhythmic sucking of her thumb, she was completely still. Content to just sit there on his lap. She didn't ask for anything or make a fuss. She wasn't the least bit afraid of him, which was maybe the weirdest thing of all.

He exhaled a breath he hadn't known he was holding and tried to relax. It wasn't easy, given that he didn't want to move.

Distraction. That was what he needed. Something to make him forget the little girl, the vulnerable scent. Unfortunately, cartoons didn't seem to be sufficient.

His thoughts turned to Hailey. Falling back on an old exercise his first partner had taught him, he did an inventory of the woman, starting from the outside and moving in.

Blond, but not the fake kind—no dark roots. He wasn't a betting man, but he'd lay his disability check on her hair not being a result of an advancement in chemistry. Her eyebrows were light, too, although not nearly as light as her hair.

Blue eyes. Almost the same color as Megan's, but not quite. Hailey's were a little darker and a little wiser. But there was innocence in the woman's eyes, too. Vulnerability. She shouldn't be involved in this mess. He just knew it. If Roy's killers knew he had a kid and they came back to clean up any loose ends…

He was digressing. Back to the exercise. What kind of skin did she have? *Soft.* No, dammit, he couldn't put that down on a report. Pale. That was better. Pale and perfect, not a wrinkle, not a scar, nothing.

Nose? Normal. Narrow. Nothing that would set her apart.

Mouth? Now that was a little more interesting. Her mouth had caught his attention a couple of times. She smiled easily and she had good teeth. White, even, like someone in a toothpaste commercial. But her lips were the nicest part of her face. The color of coral or maybe pinker than that. Pretty. A terrific smile.

How'd Captain Driscoll like to see him write that about a witness? The witness had a terrific smile and vulnerable eyes. Yeah, that would go over with a bang.

The funny thing was, she wasn't that attractive on first glance. Nothing that would stop traffic. But now that he'd talked with her, thought about her, he could see that she had her own kind of pretty. Especially when she smiled.

It didn't hurt that she had the kind of figure he most admired. Not too skinny, like those starving models, but nice. Womanly. Her curves were the real McCoy, he'd bet. None of that silicone for her.

She was the kind of woman he never dated. He didn't want apple pie and together forever. He wanted right now and out the door. At least, that was what he *had* wanted.

Now, if he was smart, he wouldn't want anything. Anybody. The women in his life had all made it perfectly clear that he wasn't required to talk much, think much or even spend much money. Because he had the muscles. Because he knew exactly what a woman wanted before she knew herself. It was his physique and his technique, the terrible duo that had been his best buddies, that had made the women come home with him. And thanks to a bullet, he no longer had either.

He'd heal, but he'd never be the same. He'd have the scars and the limp and the knowledge that he was just as vulnerable as the kid on his lap. He couldn't leap tall buildings in a single bound or outrun a speeding train, but he sure as hell could stop a bullet with his hip.

Megan shifted and he tensed again. She withdrew her wet thumb from her mouth. "Is Hailey coming back?" she asked, then popped the thumb back in.

"I sure as h— I hope so," he said.

She didn't say anything more. She just watched her show. The cat and mouse had been replaced by Bugs Bunny and Elmer Fudd. At least Jack knew who they were. Even so, Bugs wasn't enough of a distraction. All he could think about was the kid on his lap and the woman down the hall. He'd give it two more minutes, and then he'd go see what was keeping Hailey.

He only had to wait one minute. The door wasn't locked and Hailey walked in, but Jack couldn't do anything about it because Megan didn't leave. He'd figured for sure she'd jump down, but she just sat there, her head turned to the right, waiting for Hailey to come into her field of vision.

"I see you two have made yourselves comfortable."

Jack cleared his throat, sure that if he said anything at all, the kid would take it personally. He could see Hailey now, carrying two big supermarket bags, one in each arm. She'd put on a jacket. He hoped she'd take it off soon.

"How does everyone like spaghetti?" she asked, focusing on Megan.

The little girl nodded.

"Uh, you need help?" Jack asked. Praying she'd say yes.

"No, not at all. You just sit tight. I'll let you know when lunch is ready."

Not the answer he was looking for. Damn.

Hailey smiled as she put the bags on the counter. Jack's innocent question hadn't fooled her a bit. He didn't know what to make of Megan or how to get her off his lap. Big man like him, afraid of a little girl. So silly. So...endearing. Why that should be, she didn't know, but there it was. She felt a warmth from Jack she hadn't before. Perhaps because, even though he didn't want Megan on his lap, he didn't force her to leave. That said something about him. Something good.

She hung her jacket on the back of a chair, then unpacked her supplies: vegetables and fruits, milk, spaghetti noodles, sauce, some frozen dinners and some chicken she'd found in her freezer, orange juice, hot cereal and several cans of soup. Not that she planned on making all this today. But she'd probably be going to the market long before Jack did, and she wanted him to have something healthy in the house.

It only took her a few minutes to find a pot big enough for the pasta and another for the sauce; he even had a strainer, which was good. But she had to wash everything first. He clearly didn't cook often, if ever.

Poor guy. She glanced at him again, almost laughing out loud at his rigid posture. Then it occurred to her that maybe Megan was hurting him. That wasn't so amusing. "Megan, honey, want to come help me make lunch?"

Megan popped her thumb out of her mouth and solemnly climbed down from her perch. As soon as her feet touched the ground, Hailey saw Jack exhale. Such a big exhalation, in fact, she wondered if he'd breathed at all while she was gone.

As Megan approached, Hailey took the opportunity to look at her closely. Her eyes weren't red anymore; she apparently hadn't cried since the bath. But there was something different about her. The light on the inside had dimmed. She didn't shine anymore. The automatic smile wasn't there. *Please God, let it be temporary. Let her recover.*

Hailey got three plates from the cupboard and held them out to the little girl. "Can you set these on the table?"

Megan nodded, then put her doll on the floor. She took the plates and went to the table, placing the dishes right in front of the three chairs. Then she turned to wait for her next task. So quiet. So obedient. It broke Hailey's heart.

Megan ended up setting the table perfectly, down to the folded paper napkins. Hailey made a salad and

finished up the spaghetti, all the while thinking about
what she should do. Take Megan back to her place?
Probably. Despite Jack's misgivings, Hailey couldn't
imagine that whoever had killed Roy would care
much about a four-year-old girl. It would have made
her feel better, though, if she understood why Roy
had been killed. Drugs? A burglary gone bad? Fool.
Damn fool. He shouldn't have done anything dangerous, not when he had Megan in his care.

"You need a hand?"

She looked up to see Jack standing in the kitchen
by the refrigerator. She'd been so preoccupied that
she hadn't even seen him walk by. "No, no. We're
almost ready. Just a few more minutes."

He headed for one of the kitchen chairs, and
Hailey turned to Megan. "Honey, why don't you go
play for a bit? I'll call you as soon as lunch is
ready."

Megan obeyed, taking Tottie with her. Once she
was out of the room, Hailey poured the spaghetti into
the colander and ran some cool water over it. She
brought the salad to the table and sat down next to
Jack. "I've been thinking…" she said.

"Yeah?"

"About what to do next."

"Okay." His eyes narrowed slightly, as if he was
already planning to nix any ideas she might have.

"I'm going to take her back to my place," she
said. "She's comfortable there. She knows me."

"You realize you'll be questioned. And if they
find out you've got Megan, they'll call social services."

"Why would they question me?"

"Because you live in the complex. They'll question everyone."

"And if I tell them I don't know anything?"

He shook his head. "Did Chandler always pay you in cash?"

She thought about it. "Mostly. But a few times he wrote me a check."

"Did anyone else in the building know you looked after Megan?"

"Okay, I get it. They'll figure out I was her sitter."

"That's right. And they'll figure Roy left her with you."

"He didn't."

"You want me to lie?"

She took in a breath, thinking hard about what she was going to propose. "Yes, I guess I do. I want to tell the police that I haven't seen Megan. That she went to visit relatives."

"And if they ask who these relatives are?"

"I'll tell them the truth. That I don't know."

"It's too risky."

"Why? What harm can it possibly do to keep this child for a while? She's been traumatized enough without having to go downtown. Without someone putting her in a foster home with strangers."

"Hailey," he said, "I agree. It's not the best solution. But it's the only one that will keep you out of trouble."

"I don't mind trouble," she said.

He smiled at her, a kind of lopsided grin. "You've never been in trouble a day in your life."

"How do you know?"

He laughed. "All I have to do is look at you. Oh, maybe you exceeded the speed limit once. Probably had an overdue book at the library. But trouble? Uh-uh."

"Well, Mr. Know-it-all, you're wrong."

"I am?"

She nodded. "I got into some very serious trouble once."

He studied her for a moment. "How old were you?"

She felt her cheeks heat and she looked away. "Eleven."

"What'd you do—break someone's window?"

"It was a church window, thank you. And I was in trouble for a long time."

"I'll bet."

She looked at him again, at his smug little smirk. "Just because I haven't been in trouble before doesn't mean I won't be able to handle trouble now."

"I have no doubts about that. Only, it's best to avoid trouble if you can."

"But don't you see?" she asked, no longer teasing. "I can't. I love Megan, Jack. I've taken care of her for two years. She's like family. I can't give her up."

He sighed. "Let me think about it," he said. "Maybe there's another solution."

She nodded. At least it wasn't a straight-out no.

Hailey called Megan to the table, then served up lunch. It was a quiet affair, no idle chatter, not even from Megan. And when they finished, Megan put her dish on the counter like a perfect little soldier. Then she went back to the floor, to her cartoons.

"Listen," Hailey said, "I'm going to go get a few more things from my place."

He looked a little panicked. "You won't be long, will you?"

"I'll be back before you can say Sesame Street."

"Okay, then," he said, his panic softening a bit. But only a bit.

She grabbed her jacket from the chair and put it on. "I brought juice for her. It's in the fridge. But I doubt she'll want any."

He looked out to where Megan sat watching TV. Hailey went over to her and saw that her eyes were only half-open. She would be asleep very soon. Just looking at her made Hailey's heart contract, and she had to fight another bout of tears.

She went back to Jack at the table. "She's almost asleep. So don't worry."

"All right," he said. "But hurry."

"I will."

She left his apartment and headed straight for hers. She wanted it to be ready for Megan, with lots of familiar things around. But first she changed the sheets on the daybed in the guest room, and then she looked for Megan's stuffed bunny, but she couldn't find it. The room that had been fine for temporary baby-sitting looked woefully unequipped for a long stay. It wouldn't do at all.

Hailey went to her desk and got the key Roy had given her, then she picked up her empty clothes hamper to use as a carryall. As she headed outside and around to Roy's apartment, she thought about all the things she wanted to get. The bunny. Some more clothes, especially pajamas and a warm jacket. There was a picture of Roy in the living room, and Hailey wanted Megan to have that. There had to be some other things that would bring Megan comfort later on.

She reached Roy's apartment and slipped the key into the lock. The first thing she saw when she opened the door was chaos. Someone had been there. Someone searching desperately for something. Because there wasn't one piece of furniture that wasn't overturned or ripped to shreds. Not one picture that wasn't torn down the middle. Not one cabinet that wasn't opened and emptied.

Her heart started beating so fast she didn't think she could move. She wasn't going to find anything to comfort Megan here. Everything in her world had been destroyed by monsters. Real monsters. No one else could have done something this destructive.

She stepped back, pulling the door closed. Just as the lock clicked in, a hand gripped her shoulder.

Chapter Five

Hailey whipped around, slamming the clothes hamper into the stomach of her assailant. He doubled over, and she saw that he was wearing a uniform. A policeman's uniform.

"Oh, no. Oh, my God." She dropped the basket and bent over to see his face. To make sure that he was breathing and she hadn't broken something important.

His face was red, but his eyes were open and he was breathing, albeit raggedly. With his free hand on his stomach, he stood up. He looked awfully mad.

They stood like that for a few seconds. Hailey was afraid to move, even though she thought about making a run for it. But where would she go? The officer had seen her.

"I'm sorry," she said, but it sounded pathetic even to her own ears.

"Uh-huh."

"You scared me." She swallowed. "I'm really sorry."

"Not your fault," the cop said, his voice still

whispery with trauma. "I shouldn't have come up on you like that."

"Why did you?" she asked, deciding right then to act as if she knew absolutely nothing. "Is it about what happened to Roy's apartment?"

"You were inside?"

She shook her head. "I was just coming to get the laundry and I opened the door. It's awful in there. The whole place is torn up. Do you know where Roy is? Where Megan is?"

The cop, a youngish man with dark closely cropped hair and thin lips, stared at her hard. "I was going to ask you that question."

"You mean, they're gone?"

He was breathing easily again. He looked her over from top to bottom and back. "What's your name?"

"Hailey Bishop."

"You live here?"

"Yes. In 3301."

"What's your relationship to Roy Chandler?"

"I baby-sit for Megan sometimes. And I do some housework and laundry."

"When's the last time you saw Chandler?"

"About four days ago," she said, telling the truth.

"Did he say anything to you about leaving town?"

"No. Nothing. I watched Megan for a couple of hours and then he came for her. We barely said ten words."

"Huh," the cop said, still looking at her as if she might whap him with the laundry basket again.

"Listen, do you mind if I go inside?"

His brows came down. "Why?"

"I'd like to see if there's anything left in Megan's room. You know, for when she gets back. She's going to be so upset. This is an awful thing for a little girl."

"It's a crime scene," he said. "You can't go in there."

"Can't you take me? I promise, I won't touch anything without your permission." Hailey knew it was futile. No cop in his right mind would let her into an active crime scene. She'd seen enough television shows to know that. And yet, he didn't dismiss her out of hand. He just stared at her some more.

She glanced down, trying not to be too obvious. There it was. His badge. Nichols. Officer Nichols. Why wasn't he saying anything?

"All right," he said. "It's not regulation, but I'll take you in. But don't touch anything without my permission, got it?"

"Oh, thank you," she said. She smiled at him as if he'd done her a huge favor, but on the inside, she just got more frightened. Why was he breaking the rules? Would he get her inside and do something horrible? Maybe kill her or frame her for Roy's death? "You're very nice, but no. I don't want you to get in any trouble on my account. I'll just wait until…" She started backing up, little steps.

"I won't get in any trouble," he said. "I think you're right about the kid. Let's see if there's anything of hers left."

Hailey tried to find another excuse, but the cop took hold of her arm as he opened the door. She had no choice but to go in with him.

The living room was completely trashed. Whoever had done this hadn't been kidding around. They'd been looking for something, and they hadn't been shy about it.

Hailey hoped with all her heart that they'd found it. That whatever Roy had hidden had been in the apartment. But something told her they hadn't. And that Officer Nichols knew it, and figured she might point him in the right direction.

She walked quickly through the living room and down the hallway right to Megan's bedroom, Officer Nichols on her heels. The door was open, so she didn't have to wait for the verdict. Everything, including Megan's stuffed toys, was in shreds.

Despite her fear and her struggle to keep her wits about her, Hailey's eyes burned with tears as she thought of what that poor little thing was going through. Nothing left of her life but a picture, a recipe, a doll. Even that photo of Roy had been destroyed. How would Megan remember him?

"Guess there's not much to salvage, after all," Nichols said.

"No. Nothing." She turned, holding the laundry basket in front of her. "I'd better be going. I'm sure you have a lot to do here."

"You know if he had any relatives?" Nichols asked, as if she hadn't spoken.

"I think so. I'm pretty sure Roy told me he had a sister in Florida. Or was it a brother?"

"Florida?"

"I think. Maybe Georgia. I'm not sure."

"You don't have any phone numbers? In case of emergency or something like that?"

"Just the pediatrician. What happened here?" she asked, deciding to change tactics. "Who did this?"

He didn't answer her. The only move he made was to lift his hand to his leather holster and finger the big metal snap. "I think you ought to give me the key, Ms. Bishop. You won't be doing any more laundry for this family."

When she pulled the key out of her pocket, her hand shook. She handed it to the policeman, inadvertently brushing the palm of his hand. It was damp with sweat.

"You're Officer Nichols?"

He looked to his right, then back at her. Which meant, if her classes in neurolinguistic programming could be believed, he was about to tell her a lie. "That's right."

"Am I going to be questioned?"

"Someone will be in touch with you," he said, not answering her at all. "I think you'd better leave now, though."

"Yes, all right," she said, glancing back at Megan's room. She couldn't quell an involuntary shudder. "Awful," she whispered. "Just awful."

The officer stepped aside for her to pass. As she walked down the hallway, she had the horrible feeling she was going to be shot in the back. That the next second would be her last.

When she reached the living room, she started running. She didn't stop until she got to Jack's door. With a shaking hand, she turned the knob, grateful

Jack hadn't locked the door behind her. She did, however, checking the dead bolt twice.

Jack was standing in the doorway of the kitchen opening a beer. But the moment he saw her, he put the bottle down. "What's wrong?"

Hailey glanced around for Megan. Thankfully she was asleep. Hailey put down her empty basket and headed for Jack, all the while trying to calm down.

He sat and she pulled up a chair right next to him. "I went to Roy's apartment," she said.

"You *what?*"

She held up a hand to shush him. "I know, I know. But I didn't think—"

"That's right, you didn't."

"Hey," she said, indignation making her pulse accelerate again. "Pardon me for not being up on my murder-investigation etiquette."

"It's not etiquette I'm worried about. It's blundering into a situation that could get you killed."

She couldn't really argue with him. What if the person who'd trashed the apartment had still been there? She shuddered, thinking it was quite scary enough, thank you.

"Well?"

"The place was a wreck. Not untidy. Slashed to bits. Nothing was left intact, and I mean nothing. Not even the pictures on the wall."

Jack didn't comment, but she could see his jaw muscles flex. He'd shaved. He must have done that just after she'd gone. He looked nice without the stubble.

"Is there more?"

She glanced away, flustered to have been caught like that. Curious, too. Why, when her heart was still beating like a drum, would she pause to think about his face?

"Hailey?"

She closed her eyes for a second. When she opened them again, she was able to focus more clearly. "There was a policeman there."

"Inside?"

She shook her head. "No. Outside. He stopped me just after I opened the door."

Jack nodded slowly. "He was alone?"

"As far as I could tell. I didn't see anyone else."

"No tape in his hand, no camera?"

"Nothing. His name was Nichols, according to his name tag."

Jack leaned back. "Brett Nichols?"

"I didn't ask his first name. But something was peculiar about him."

"What?"

"He let me go inside. Actually, he pretty much insisted."

"What?"

"I know. It struck me as very odd. I mean, why would he want me to go inside, unless he figured I might lead him to...whatever they were looking for."

"Nichols. I've heard the name."

"Thin lips," she said. "Really short hair, a military cut. Tall, but not as tall as you. And really long fingers."

"Long fingers?" Jack repeated.

"Yeah. Like he should have been a piano player, instead of a cop."

"Uh-huh," Jack said, clearly not thrilled with her description, which wasn't fair at all. It was very accurate. She'd be able to pick him out of a lineup in a flash.

Jack rubbed his chin as he thought about what Hailey was telling him. If Nichols was on the level, he'd have a lot of explaining to do. No way he should have let her go into that apartment. It compromised the whole scene.

So what was he doing there? And where was the rest of the crime team?

He saw that Hailey had calmed down. At least her breathing seemed normal. She took off her jacket and flung it casually over the back of the far chair. As if she'd been here often. As if she knew him.

"You know what else? He didn't seem all that surprised about the house. As if it was no big deal that every single thing had been torn apart."

"How do you know he didn't do the tearing?" Jack asked.

She stopped. Blinked. Her pretty coral lips turned up into a smile and her eyes lit up. "Of course! *He* did it," she said, as if she'd scooped the *New York Times*. "He did it wearing a policeman's uniform, so if anyone came by, he could just say he was there to make a report or something. I bet he wasn't a real cop at all."

"Don't bust your arm patting yourself on the back," Jack said. "We don't know who he is. Or if he did anything. He might have been looking for the people who tore up the place. It seems pretty likely that he was looking for whatever the killer had been looking for.''

''Or maybe he *is* the killer.''

''Maybe,'' he said, kind of liking the way she was smiling at him. The way her cheeks were flushed with excitement. How she'd told him the facts without getting all emotional. She'd remembered details, and that was good. But he knew she didn't get it. She didn't get that this wasn't a game, and that the stakes were life and death. Here they were, talking about murder suspects and bogus cops, and she was as excited as a kid climbing on a roller coaster. But he knew the kind of ride she could expect if she hung on. Roller coasters are only fun because there's no real danger.

''I'd better get Megan up,'' Hailey said. ''I'm worried that she's sleeping so much.''

''I want you two to stay here tonight,'' he said.

She nodded. ''I think that's a good idea. But what about after tonight? After tomorrow night?''

''I don't know.''

''I've got a question.'' She stood up, but put her hands on the back of the chair. ''How come you aren't more surprised?''

''About what?''

''About me running into that cop. Or about what he did?''

''I am surprised.''

She shook her head. ''Nope. When I told you what had happened, you nodded. As if you'd expected something like that. You found out something at the police station, didn't you?''

He sighed. He'd been right about her. She was nosy. Nosy and intuitive, and too eager for her own good. He'd have to be careful with her. She could get herself into a lot of trouble, and he wasn't going to be able to get her out of it.

"Come on, Jack. Tell me. I have a right to know."

"No, you don't," he said. "But I'm going to tell you, anyway."

She sat back down again and leaned forward, waiting.

"When I did the background check on Roy, I found out that he used to work for Craig Faraday."

"From UTI? That big computer company?"

Jack nodded, wondering if he was doing the right thing by misdirecting her. But what good would it do for him to tell her the truth? If the cops were involved, he'd find out. But he still wasn't convinced it had anything to do with the police department.

"He and his wife. Chandler changed his name after being fired for stealing."

"So you think that whatever he stole is what they were looking for?"

"Makes sense to me." Jack heard a little squeak behind him. A noise unlike any he'd heard before. It was the girl of course, but he couldn't imagine why she'd made that high-pitched sound. "What's that?"

"That was a very tiny girl yawning," Hailey said, rising once more. She smiled as she turned to walk away.

Jack got up, too, and picked up the beer he'd put

down when Hailey had come back. He made his way over to his chair, but he didn't sit right away. Instead, he watched her reflection on the television screen. He saw her open her arms wide as she knelt on the quilt. Megan crawled into her lap, curling herself into a little ball. As soon as Hailey's arms went around her, the kid put her thumb back in her mouth and closed her eyes.

To be that comfortable in someone's arms was something he didn't understand. He got the concept of course, and he saw the truth of it right there on the screen, but it was foreign to him all the same. He'd found many things in the arms of a woman, but never safety. Never that kind of comfort. He'd never had that much trust in anyone.

"Did you and Tottie sleep well?" Hailey asked.

Megan's head moved up and down, but the thumb didn't leave her mouth.

"How about, when you wake up a little bit more, we play a game?"

Again the little head bobbed.

"And then you can help me fix dinner. Because guess what? We're all going to sleep here tonight. A big slumber party! Won't that be fun?"

Megan didn't nod this time, and Jack figured she was thinking about where she should be sleeping. Her own bed. With her toys and dolls all around her. Did she know it was over? A kid that age, could she grasp the notion of a world turned upside down? Probably. The kids he'd run across in his years on the force had all been savvy as hell. Dangerous and devious, too, but the truth was they all understood much more than most people gave them credit for.

Despite Hailey's belief that it would take Megan a while to come to terms with Roy's death, he knew the kid got it. All the sleeping, well, that was because she didn't like it. And because she didn't know what to do with it. But she knew. She knew she'd never go home again.

"I have to go potty."

Jack shook his head. Kids. Strange little creatures.

He watched Hailey and Megan get up and walk out of range. The television was dark again. He closed his eyes and listened to Hailey's voice. He wasn't even sure what she was saying, but the way she said it made him relax. No wonder Megan had climbed so willingly into her arms.

The bathroom door closed, cutting off the sound. He looked at his watch. It was almost two, and he hadn't gone over the rest of the material from his morning visit to the station. He'd forwarded a bunch of files to his home computer. He put his beer down and headed for his bedroom.

His hip had stopped throbbing, but he grimaced as he walked, anticipating the stabs of pain he'd almost grown accustomed to. But it wasn't nearly as intense as he'd prepared for.

He probably should have been doing those exercises the physical therapist had given him. She'd told him it would help, but he'd figured she was full of crap. It was hard to imagine, but maybe he'd been mistaken. Maybe he wasn't destined to live the life of a cripple.

No. Better not start thinking that way. It would
only get him into trouble. He'd never be whole again,
and no amount of leg lifts was going to change that.

As he passed the bathroom door, he heard laughter. Feminine. Womanly. A good sound.

But then he got to his room and saw his neatly-
made bed. Fresh sheets, too. He wished she hadn't
done that. It made him uncomfortable to think she'd
seen the way he'd been living. She probably thought
he was a huge slob. Hell, he'd become a real slob.
It was the damn hip, that was all. But she wouldn't
know that. She'd think he always lived like this.

He shook the depressing thoughts away and
grabbed the laptop from his dresser. She designed
web sites. Maybe he'd find hers by doing a search
for her name. She was probably very talented. Pity
he hadn't met her six months ago.

Chapter Six

Hailey put away the last of the dinner dishes and checked on Jack and Megan. The two of them were in his chair again, this time watching *The Simpsons*. She wasn't sure either one of them liked it that much, if their expressions were anything to go by. Megan watched little Maggie, mirroring the thumb-sucking movement for movement. Jack seemed perplexed by the whole show, and she wondered if he'd ever seen it before.

"This is for kids?" he asked when she joined them in the living room.

"No, actually it's also for adults. I like it. It's silly, but there're some very sophisticated jokes in there, too."

"Uh-huh," he said, looking at her with that same perplexed gaze.

"And I suppose all you watch is PBS and the Discovery channel?"

He grinned. "ESPN, too. But only for the social commentary."

"You're an only child, right?"

"How'd you guess?" he asked, his gaze following her all the way to the couch.

"I'm not sure. Just a feeling."

He shifted unconsciously so that Megan's head fell more naturally on his shoulder. "You're a middle child. Right?"

She nodded. "Yeah."

"I figured," he said. "You take care of people. I read that's a trait of middle children."

"That's not all I do."

"No, but it's what comes naturally to you. You want to make things comfortable."

"I know. I'm trying to break the habit, but—"

"Are you kidding?"

"No. It's not such a great trait to have."

"Really? Want to ask Megan about that?"

Hailey smiled.

Megan looked up at Jack's chin, then back to Bart and Lisa.

"Okay, so it's not as bad as some things. But it's gotten me into situations..."

He waited patiently while she wondered why she was about to share so much. The answer didn't come. "The men I've chosen haven't been very good for me. I let them take advantage."

"I can see that. I can see where a man would want to sit back and let you carry the load."

"The worst part about it is that I'm so predictable," she said, leaning back on his couch, letting her shoulders relax. "I wanted to be rebellious. It was a disaster. There was nothing exciting about it. Nothing daring. I just did the opposite of what I felt

I should do, but that's being controlled just the same.''

"You seemed pretty darn rebellious this afternoon.''

"I did?''

"Most folks wouldn't have gone to that apartment.''

"That wasn't rebellious. That was stupid.''

He chuckled, making Megan's hair tremble. "Yeah, that, too.''

"So what now, Detective?'' she asked, and by her wince, she'd realized her mistake the moment the word was out of her mouth.

"Sleep,'' he said, determined not to show that her slip had made him uncomfortable. He wasn't a detective anymore, and he probably wouldn't be again. But that wasn't her fault. "We'll figure out what's next in the morning.''

"I'm not ready for bed yet,'' she said. "It's too early.''

He stared at the burger commercial for a long while, then turned back to her. "I don't have a lot of things to do in here.''

"Television is fine.''

"I have a couple of books in the bedroom,'' he said.

Hailey shook her head, then curled her legs under her and focused on the TV. Even though she watched the show, she could tell his gaze was on her. It wasn't like this afternoon, when she'd felt Officer Nichols's eyes on her back. This was a different kind of watchfulness. One she didn't seem to mind, except that she had the urge to fix her hair.

What kind of man was he? she wondered. A loner. A rogue. But there was a gentleness about him that pulled him out of the little box she wanted to put him in. It was clear he didn't know what to do with Megan, and yet... She turned and her gaze met his.

So dark, those eyes. With those sinfully long lashes. So full of mystery. Shuttered, but not as tightly as he'd like to believe. There was vulnerability there. And kindness. But more than that, she sensed a helplessness in him. Which was foreign territory, that much she knew for sure. The man had never been helpless before. He'd always come to the rescue of those who were.

Who would rescue him?

Not her. Not with her weaknesses. Her struggle to be independent. He needed someone strong, of heart, of character, of mind.

He looked away slowly, moving his head to force his gaze from hers. It made her conscious of how deeply she'd looked at him, how she hadn't hidden her curiosity at all. "Jack?"

"Yeah?"

"Is this how it's supposed to feel?"

"What?" he asked, his eyes on the TV now.

"I don't know. I guess you're used to it, but it's my first time being this close to—"

"I'm not used to it."

"It's surreal. Like it happened on the *X-Files* or something. I've never been scared like that before. And frankly, I don't ever want to be again."

"You kept your head," he said, finally looking at her. "You did great."

"I suppose it's good to know that I won't fall apart or faint."

"Hell, I would have."

She smiled. "You lie like a rug."

"Ouch," he said. "You've got a sharp tongue there, missy."

Her smile faded as her gaze moved to the little girl on his lap. "It'll never be the same again, will it?"

"No," he said, and she knew he'd gotten her meaning. "It won't. That's not to say it won't be good. It'll just be different."

"I need for it to be good. I don't think I could handle things at all if I thought it was going to get worse."

"Don't think so much."

"Is that how you get by? You don't think about it?"

"That's the goal," he said, his voice suddenly weary. "I don't succeed nearly as much as I'd like."

"I'm not sure that's the answer," she said.

"Maybe not. But it's the only one I've got."

She sighed, then rubbed her temples with her fore-fingers where the beginning of a headache was sneaking up on her.

"You okay?"

She nodded. Then she leaned her head back on the couch cushion and closed her eyes.

"Hailey."

She opened her eyes. Jack stood in front of her, his hand on her shoulder. "What?" she asked.

"You fell asleep. About two hours ago. But you're gonna be stiff in the morning if you stay here all night. Why don't you go on to bed? You can sleep in my room." He gave her a half smile. "The sheets are clean."

"I'll be fine out here."

He shook his head. "I'm used to this. I mostly sleep in the chair."

"Which is probably why you hurt so badly. Come on, Jack," she said, standing, stretching her arms way over her head. "You go on into your room. I can see you're as wiped out as I am."

He started to protest, but she held up a hand to stop him. "I want to be near Megan," she said. She looked at the floor where Megan had spread her quilt. She needed a blanket, but other than that, she was good for the night.

"We can put her in the bedroom."

"No. And that's the end of it." She went to the hall closet and took out the extra set of sheets and two blankets. She dropped her things on the couch, then put the other blanket over Megan, making sure she was all covered up.

Megan stirred, then opened her eyes. "Hailey?"

"Yes, honey?"

"Is it time for my bedtime story?"

Hailey smiled. "One story, and then it's back to sleep."

Megan looked up at Jack, then back at her. So sweet. So helpless. Like a kitten weaned too early. Hailey's heart ached as she sat on the floor and began to tell the story of Sleeping Beauty.

Jack listened to her for a long time. He sat on the arm of the couch, then about ten minutes later, moved to the cushion. The story wasn't exactly new to him, but the way Hailey told it was. Her voice alone could have soothed a whole psych ward. When she described the baby in the story, she made it sound exactly like Megan. He found himself smiling as Hailey used silly accents for the three fairy godmothers.

But he didn't want to fall asleep on the couch, and if he listened any longer, he would. So he hoisted himself up, the throb in his hip a part of him now. He took his pills and headed for the hallway. But he stopped once more and looked back at Megan. Her eyes were closed, and as he watched, her little wet thumb fell out of her mouth.

Hailey bent down and kissed the girl on her forehead and then on her nose. She tucked her in again to keep her warm and then stood up. "I didn't think you were still awake."

"I won't be for long." He took a step, then stopped again. "Are you sure I can't persuade you to let me sleep out here?"

She shook her head. "Nope."

He sighed. "Have it your own way."

She frowned slightly as she moved toward the couch. "You wouldn't happen to have any pajamas I could borrow, do you?"

"I think that can be arranged."

"I'll get them," she said. "If you'll tell me where they are."

He was too tired to argue with her. "Third drawer down. And no peeking at my underwear."

Her soft laughter lingered in the room after she'd gone down the hall. It had been too long since he'd had a woman's laughter in this dump. But he better not get used to it. He made his way into the bathroom to get ready for bed, wondering all the while what pajamas she'd choose. He had quite a selection. His aunt in Rhode Island sent him a pair every year for Christmas. Most of them were simple cotton, but there was this one pair that was made out of something real clingy. The image of her in them spurred him to finish his nightly routine in half the time. But when he came out to say good-night, he saw she'd picked the plain old navy blue ones. Now if she'd left the bottoms in the drawer...

"I'll turn off the lights," she said. "Is there anything else you need? A glass of water for the nightstand?"

"I was just on my way to get it."

"I'll go. You go get ready."

"Damn middle child," he said, giving her one of his best scowls.

"Sticks and stones, Jack. Sticks and stones."

She actually beat him to his room. As he walked in, she was putting down the glass with one hand and picking up his physical-therapy papers with the other.

"These look tough," she said. "I don't think I could do half of them."

"That's supposed to be a routine specific to my injuries and my physical condition at the time of the accident," he said. "It's all a bunch of crap if you ask me."

"You don't do them?" she asked.

"I do enough."

She frowned. "I'll bet."

"Go to bed, middle child," he said. "You've saved enough of the world today."

She put the papers back down, causing the pajama sleeve to straighten and her hand to completely disappear. She looked like a little kid in his clothes. Except, of course, for the curve of her breasts.

"What are you smiling at?"

"Nothing."

She sniffed her disbelief, then walked past him. But she didn't make it out the door quite yet. She stopped, turned back. "Thank you," she said.

"For what?"

"For not sending Megan away."

He nodded. Sending Megan to family services was the least of their problems. He had a lot of digging to do tomorrow. A lot of answers to find. But he had to admit that he'd sleep easier knowing the kid was safe with Hailey.

THE AWARENESS *that someone was in the room came slowly to him. A sound, a moan. No. That was his voice.*

There.

A step. A creak from the floor.

He was lying on his stomach, and now his hand slid slowly up the bed past his face, under the pillow,

finding the welcome hard grip of his .357. He eased
the safety off without opening his eyes.

*Another move. The bed dipping with the weight of
the intruder… Hailey. It's Hailey. The neighbor. The
woman.*

*Her hand on his shoulder. Delicate. Warm. Ten-
tative. Moving now, down his back, to the small of
his back where the pain centered before it radiated
down his legs.*

*Slight pressure. The palm of her hand in a tight
circle. Deeper now. Rubbing. Warm.*

He moaned.

"Shh," she said, her voice as soft as the touch of
her palm.

"What are you doing?"

"You were in pain," she said. "I heard you from
the other room."

"A pill," he said, moving to get up.

Her hand stilled. Stopped him. "In a minute," she
whispered. "Let me help."

He hesitated as her hand began to circle once
again. Little by little she increased the pressure, a
mixture of pain and pleasure, but with each movement the pain eased and the pleasure increased. The
throbbing in his hip eased, too. All his concentration
went to her hand, and the skin and muscle beneath
her hand, and then to the sound of her breathing, the
heat of her thigh touching his thigh.

"Let it go," she said, her voice a low murmur.
"Let the pain go with each breath. Picture yourself
somewhere you love. The mountains. The ocean.

Your shoulders relax. With each breath, the tension slips away.''

Her other hand was on his back. Both hands were moving, rubbing. Just the right place, the right pressure. The touch itself so welcome to flesh that had been so long without it.

Her words continued but had no meaning. Just the sound entering his head and snaking down to meet her hands. All his focus on her palms, on her heat.

And then, a slow awareness of his legs, and his arms and shoulders. As if he'd been somewhere outside and had just now slipped back inside.

An awareness of her, too. The way she made the bed dip. Her voice, like smoke swirling around him and inside him. Her scent. Womanly, sweet.

Her hands moved up to his shoulder blades and she increased the pressure. He moaned again, feeling the first relief in days, months. Her heat healing him, and waking him. Waking a part of him that had been dormant. Stirring his thoughts away from his body and on to hers.

"Relax," she said. "You tensed up again."

He fought to bring his focus back to his muscles. But it was no good. He couldn't turn his mind away from the picture of her hair, and her eyes, and the curves of her body.

Her hands on his neck, on his bare skin. It was too much, too real, and his body, the long dormant part of him, stirred. He didn't want it to happen, and he struggled to disengage again, but then she ran her hand, her splayed fingers, through his hair. She leaned over, and he could feel the softness of her breast brush his arm.

He moved, torn between the hell of his reaction and the heaven of her touch. He wanted her hands somewhere else. He wanted her lips on his. He wanted to feel her underneath him. As a woman. Not as a neighbor. Not as a nurse.

He moaned again, and she leaned down, pressing her breast against his back.

"Shh."

"No," he said, embarrassed and flustered. He had no business getting aroused. He didn't know her. She wasn't coming on to him. She was trying to be nice. To help.

"Please," he said, forcing himself to sound calm. "It's no good."

Her hands lifted. "Am I hurting you?"

"No," he said. "It's not you."

"I don't understand."

He took a deep breath, grateful for the darkness in his room. "I know. Don't worry. You didn't do anything wrong. I just need to take a pill now."

She didn't move for a few seconds. Even though he knew she wasn't touching him, the feel of her palms were imprinted on his flesh.

"I'm sorry," she whispered.

"No, don't," he said. "I feel better. Honestly. It was—"

"I'll see you in the morning," she said.

"Hailey, wait."

"Good night."

The bed moved, the floor creaked, and then the

door shut. She was gone. He'd chased her away. But the effect of her hadn't gone at all. Her scent lingered. The echo of her voice still played in his mind.

It had been months since he'd felt this. Since he'd been aroused. Part of him had believed he'd never feel this again.

It would have been easier if he hadn't.

He'd been more dead than alive for a long time. At home with his anguish and his anger. Drowning in his isolation. But then Hailey had come. Not just to his place, but past his defenses.

She'd made him feel again. Made him remember he was a man. A broken man.

Chapter Seven

Hailey woke up before Megan, which worried her. Megan had always been an early riser, and with all the sleep she'd had yesterday she surely wasn't tired. But she was scared and bewildered, and Hailey had the feeling that her body was trying to protect her by making her rest. Things would go back to normal when…

When would things go back to normal? Never, for Megan, and quite possibly never for Hailey, either. Because she'd made her decision last night. She was going to keep Megan. Adopt her, if it was at all possible. But even if it wasn't, Hailey wasn't going to budge. As long as Megan didn't have a loving relative, Hailey would do whatever she had to to keep the little girl with her. To help her through this horrible loss and then help her grow up. Being single wasn't the best way to parent, but loving Megan would make up for a lot.

Of course, she'd have to convince Jack that she was doing the right thing. That would come later, though. Today, she just wanted to make sure Megan

was safe. How she was going to accomplish this
wasn't clear yet, but with Jack's help they'd find a
way.

She got up from the couch and went to the kitchen.
She put on a pot of coffee, then turned back to the
living room. Megan, wrapped in her quilt, was fine
for the moment. It didn't sound as if Jack was up
yet. She'd be back before anyone noticed.

First, though, she needed a key to Jack's apartment. She tiptoed down the hall and opened his door
a smidge, just so she could sneak a quick look. He
was sound asleep, his covers kicked off and the pillow on the floor. That must have been some rough
night. She should never have gone in, never have
tried to help. It was clear she'd just made things
worse.

She crept inside and spotted his wallet and keys
on top of the dresser. Very cautiously she picked up
the keys, then tiptoed out of the room again, closing
the door behind her.

She went back to the living room and put on her
jacket over his pajamas, then slipped on her shoes
and went outside. It was cold, close to freezing, and
the sky was gun metal gray. Nothing stirred. No
birds, no cars, nothing. She locked the door behind
her, then hurried down the walk to her apartment, the
feeling of being watched terribly acute and terribly
frightening. She tried to convince herself that it was
nonsense, but she didn't relax again until she was in
her own apartment with the dead bolt snugly in place.

Breathing easily again, she headed for her room.
She wanted to gather some clothes together, and she

wanted to shower. She'd been thinking about going to Galveston, to her parents' summer place. On the way, she could go to the mall and buy Megan some clothes and toys. They could stay out at the island until things calmed down. Until someone found Roy's killer.

She took off her jacket and pushed open her bedroom door, thinking about what she'd pack. She wasn't sure how long she'd be gone, but a few well-chosen pieces would work. There was a washer and dryer at the Galveston place, so that wouldn't be a problem. The only thing that might be a problem was her work. She'd take her laptop, but there was only one phone line out there. Not the worst thing in the world, but inconvenient.

It took her a few moments to gather up her clothes for today. Jeans, a sweatshirt, thick socks. Then she headed for the shower.

Her mind raced as she turned on the water. She needed to shave her legs. Normally she skipped that little chore during the winter.

About to take off the pajamas, she saw a shape out of the corner of her eye. A big hulk of a man with no face. He lunged for her and she fell forward, bracing herself on her hands at the last second. The hot water from the shower stung her face and drenched her back.

Just as she struggled upright, he hit her on the back of the neck, hard, and she cried out, forced down once more. She groped for something, anything, to defend herself. Her hand touched the edge of her safety razor.

He grabbed her around the waist and lifted her up as if she were nothing more than a child. It was then she realized he had a ski mask on. His dark hooded eyes and his fleshy lips were all that were visible. It wasn't the man from last night. This one was harder, stronger. And about to kill her.

"Where is she?"

"Who?"

He turned, taking her with him, and she grabbed the shower door to stop him, but he ripped her away with no effort at all. Tightening her grip on the razor's shaft, she waited until he started to put her down, then turned with all her fury and slashed at the face mask.

He jerked back, avoiding the razor, and grabbed her wrist. The force of his hand made her scream again, and with all her strength and all her will, she brought her knee up right into his crotch, slamming him with everything she had.

He let go, howling as he bent over. She ran out of the bathroom straight to the door. The lock wouldn't open. Her fingers shook too much. She tried and tried, listening to him leave the bathroom…reach the living room…come at her fast.

Finally the dead bolt clicked open and she ran outside, trying to shut the door behind her. No good. He was already there. Two steps, one step behind her.

"No!" she screamed, and stopped dead. Then, "911! 911!" she screamed, as loudly as she ever had or ever would.

She brought her hands up, curling them into tight fists, just as she'd learned in self-defense classes. She braced her feet, prepared to slam the base of her hand right in his face—right at his nose.

But then the door to her left opened. "What on earth—?"

"Help me, Gary. Call the police!"

"I've got a gun!"

"Get it!"

Her attacker froze. She could see his dark eyes look her up and down, then look at the slightly open door of her neighbor's apartment. The bastard obviously didn't care to find out if Gary really did have a gun, because he turned and ran down the walkway, past her apartment, to the stairs at the far end of the complex. She thought about following him, but she wouldn't have caught him. Not in her bare feet. Not in Jack's pajamas.

"Hailey, my God!"

She looked at her neighbor, Gary Daggett, still standing behind his door. "Thank you," she said, her voice shaky and breathless.

"Who was he?"

"I don't know."

"Well, the police will find him."

She nodded, then realized what was about to happen. The police were coming. They'd find Megan. They'd take her away. Hailey bolted toward Jack's apartment and banged on the door. She'd left the key in *her* place of course.

It was Megan who let her in. The girl's eyes widened dramatically as soon as she got a load of Hailey's wet hair and bare feet.

Then a masculine voice came from behind Megan. "What the hell?"

She looked up. Jack stood in the hallway, staring at her. He was still in his pajamas, his hair a mess, his chin dark with stubble. She wanted to tell him what had happened, but she couldn't. Her mouth didn't work. All she seemed to be able to do was shiver.

Jack headed for her, his concern growing with each labored step. When he reached her, he dropped his cane, putting both hands on her arms. "What happened?"

She opened her mouth, but nothing came out. Jack pulled her close, wrapping his arms tightly around her. She clung to him, trying to get a grip. They had to hurry and leave. There was no time.

"Was it the same guy?" he asked, his voice so close to her ear she jumped a little.

"No," she said, finally managing to speak, even though she didn't sound like herself. "Someone else."

"Did you get a look at him?"

"Mask. He had on a ski mask."

"Did he hurt you?"

That did it. The tears of fear and relief and God knew what else pooled in her eyes and ran down her face.

"Oh, jeez, he hurt you," Jack said, pulling back to look at her.

She shook her head. "No, I'm fine," she said, wiping her eyes with the sleeve of his pajamas. "But we have to go."

"Go?"

"I have a place. We have to get her out of here."

He looked at Megan, then back at Hailey. "What happened?"

"I'll tell you in the car. Just please, go pack. I'll get Megan ready."

"What about you?"

"I don't think he's in my apartment now. We'll go back together and I'll put some things in a suitcase. I left your keys there, and mine, too."

"Okay," he said. "Are you sure you're all right?"

"No, I'm not. But I will be once we get out of here."

Jack hesitated another moment, his concern making the lines bracketing his mouth seem deeper. But he let her go, got his cane and headed for his bedroom. She turned her attention to Megan, picking her up and taking her and her pillowcase of things into the bathroom. Grateful beyond all measure that Jack hadn't argued with her. That he'd listened to her urgency and adopted her plan in an instant. She'd expected something else. An argument. A dismissal.

It only took them twenty minutes to get everything together. Hailey went without her shower and put on yesterday's clothes. She'd bathe at the beach house. Her example made Jack skip his shave, although he took a mug of coffee with him.

She led them to her apartment, which was open of course. Jack made her wait while he went inside first, his cane in his left hand, his gun in his right. It was a frightening few minutes, waiting for him to come back. Hailey hadn't understood real fear before this.

But in the past two days she'd had more than her fair share. Megan, the poor thing, was fussy, probably because she'd picked up Hailey's nervousness.

Jack finally came back to the front door and gave her the all clear. She put Megan down, rushed inside and grabbed the two sets of keys. When she returned to Jack, she said, "Take her down, please. I have a van, the blue one, at the corner of the parking lot. You know where that old mattress is? Behind the pillar?"

Jack nodded as he lifted his duffel bag and put the strap over his shoulder. "I know where it is. But I don't want to leave you here."

"I know. But I'll only be two minutes. I'll be down before you have a chance to unlock the car."

He shook his head. "Someone might be down there. You keep Megan with you."

She shivered as his point hit home. "Okay." Then she smiled as brightly as she could and took Megan's hand. "Come on, sweetie. We're going to pack."

"I want to go home," she said, pulling on Hailey's hand. "I want my daddy."

"I know you do, honey," Hailey said. Every part of her wanted to hurry, to ignore Megan and pretend that it didn't matter. But she couldn't. She crouched down so Megan could look her in the eyes. "I know you want to go home, but I have a very special favor to ask you."

Megan, frowning, hugging Tottie to her tightly, didn't answer. But she didn't say no, either.

"I have to go to the beach. Have you ever been to the beach?"

Megan shook her head.

"It's very beautiful there. With lots of seashells to pick up and sand castles to build. I was hoping you would come and keep me company. Would you like to do that?"

Megan stared at her for an impossibly long time, and it was all Hailey could do to keep still. She could hear Jack's uneven footsteps as he headed toward the back stairs, and behind that, faintly, she heard a siren.

"What do you say, Megan?"

"All right."

"Wonderful! Now, here's the trick. We have to pack lickety-split. It's a race! Will you help?"

Before Megan's head stopped bobbing, Hailey was on her feet, lifting Megan into her arms. She rushed inside, straight back to her bedroom and set the girl down on her comforter. "You stay right there," she said.

Moving faster than she ever had in her life, Hailey got her suitcase open and dumped her clothes inside. Underwear, pajamas, socks, sweats. She was indiscriminate in her hurry. She got sweaters and sweatshirts from the closet, another pair of shoes and some slippers. Then she forced the suitcase closed and hoisted it off the bed. Before she left her room, she grabbed her laptop and her purse.

The siren was really near now, so she ignored her toiletries. There were plenty of drugstores in Galveston, so whatever she didn't bring, she'd buy. Urging Megan along, she carried the suitcase, computer and purse to the front door, then outside. It took her another minute to lock up, and then she practically ran down the walkway, ignoring the weight of her belongings. Megan trotted right behind.

They made it to the bottom of the stairs just as a police car turned into the parking lot. Without looking behind her, Hailey ran toward the van. Jack was behind the wheel, the engine was running and the side door was open. She threw her suitcase in, followed by the laptop and, finally, Megan. She buckled the little girl into her car seat, then closed the door behind her. ''Go,'' she said.

Jack hit the gas, knocking her sideways into the backseat. But she wasn't hurt. Just grateful that they'd made it. That the police hadn't seen them leave. That she was alive.

''Where am I going?'' Jack asked.

''To I-45. Galveston.''

''What's there?''

''My parents have a summer place.''

He nodded, turning onto Bellaire, toward the freeway.

She looked at him, gaining strength from his composure. He acted as if this was just a ride around the block. Maybe for him it was, but for her? She didn't have whatever it took to wave off the kind of morning she'd just been through. No one had ever tried to hurt her before. And she'd certainly never imagined that she'd run from the police, instead of to them. She climbed into the front seat and fastened her seat belt. ''Jack?''

''Yeah?''

''I was right, wasn't I?''

''What do you mean?''

"The police are involved."

He glanced over, his features still calm and steady. No reaction. And no denial.

"You should have told me to wait back there. You should have been on the phone to the police yourself. But here you are."

The corner of his lip lifted in a small sardonic grin. "Here I am."

"So what's going on?"

He shook his head.

"Come on, Jack. I think almost getting killed twice gives me the right to know."

He glanced back at Megan, which made Hailey look back, too. The little girl sat staring out the window, holding on to her doll and her blanket, sucking her thumb. She looked achingly small and helpless.

"I don't know what's going on," he said, keeping his voice low. "Not for sure."

"What do you think?"

He pulled behind a garbage truck at a signal, the traffic heavy even at this early hour. "I saw what happened," he said. "And I'm pretty damn sure there was an unmarked vice car involved."

"You mean...?"

He nodded. "I don't know who it was. Or if I'm even right."

"But what Nichols did yesterday gives your theory some credence."

"Yeah, it does."

She sat back, her gaze fixing on the yellow Volkswagen next to the van. The woman behind the wheel was putting on mascara as she drove. "So what are we going to do?"

"I'm going to get you two settled at this house in Galveston. And then I'm going to figure out exactly what's going on."

"How?"

"What do you mean, how? I'm a detective. My body might be shot to hell, but my mind still functions."

"Don't get your shorts in a twist. I wasn't implying anything."

"No?"

"No. I'm curious. I want to know what you plan to do, that's all."

He gave her another glance, then signaled his turn onto the Southwest Freeway. Once he'd made the turn, he ignored her until they were in the fast lane. "I don't know what I'm planning to do," he said. "I haven't figured it out yet."

"Fair enough," she said. "But, Jack?"

"Yeah?"

"You're not going to leave us, are you?"

"You'll be fine."

The panic that had just started to ebb slammed back into high gear. "Oh, no. No, no. We will not be fine. We most definitely will not be fine."

"No one knows where you're going."

"I wouldn't care if we went to the moon. I can't do this alone, Jack."

The only move he made was to look at the rear-view mirror.

"You knocked on my door, remember?" she said.

He still didn't acknowledge her.

"Jack? Really now, the least you could do—"

"Hold on tight," he said, his voice cutting into her like a knife. Then he turned the wheel sharply, sending the van careening toward the right lane, toward the exit ramp.

The scream built up in her throat as she held on to the seat for dear life. When she was finally able to look behind her to check on Megan, she saw the white car behind them, obviously following. She heard the furious honks and the squeal of brakes. She saw that the man behind the wheel had on a ski mask.

The van veered to the right, skidding out of control.

The scream broke through.

Chapter Eight

When Hailey screamed, Jack realized he was scaring his passengers to death, but he had no choice. He swerved around a Saturn and then past an old clunker, easing up on the gas as he took the sharp left at the end of the off-ramp.

Checking his rearview mirror, he saw the white car trying to make the turn, but the driver hadn't had enough time to sufficiently slow the car and the turn went wide. Wide enough that he spun out. A rending crash interrupted the honking horns as Jack straightened the wheel. He ran through a yellow light, then turned into an alleyway, slowing the van as he dodged Dumpsters and empty boxes.

At the end of the alley, he turned right, went a block, then turned left. The white car was nowhere to be seen.

He glanced behind to check on Megan. She seemed okay. Scared, but not hurt. It was a good thing her doll wasn't a little sister, though, because she held it by the neck so tightly he thought the thing would break.

Then he checked on Hailey. Her hands still clutched the seat, her knuckles white with the tension. Her neck muscles were taut as bowstrings, and her eyes were wide open. But she didn't seem hurt, either. "You okay?"

She shook her head stiffly.

"Are you hurt?"

Again she shook her head. "I really hope someone was following us," she said in a little high voice. "'Cause if not, you're pulling over right now and I'm driving."

He smiled. And relaxed. If she could joke, she was fine. "Don't worry, just because I'm paranoid, it doesn't mean someone wasn't really following us."

She turned to Megan. "Honey? You okay?"

Jack watched Megan in the rearview mirror. She nodded once, but the truth was he needed to get both of these ladies somewhere safe, and fast. It was still a good forty-minute drive to Galveston. "You want to stop somewhere? Maybe get some breakfast?"

"No," Hailey said. "I want to get out of here. I don't like that they know what kind of car I drive. Probably have the license-plate number, too."

"Yeah," he said, pulling into the parking lot of a gas station and stopping. "This house we're going to—who owns it?"

"My parents."

"Hmm. That's not so good. They can trace the car, get your name, then do a search on it."

"No," Hailey said, her gaze still on Megan. "Their name is Rogers. It's my mother's third marriage."

"So there's no connection between you? You're not on any of the mortgage papers?"

Her gaze went to him. "They could find that out?"

He nodded. "They have the law behind them. And believe me, if they really are cops, then they know all the tricks."

She shook her head. "No. There's no way they can connect me to the Galveston house."

"Okay," he said. "One more thing..."

She looked as if she didn't want to hear it.

"If you need any money, we have to get it now. While we're still at this end of town. You won't be able to use your credit cards or your checks for a while."

"All right. I'm with Bank One. Why don't we find an ATM? I need to pick up some things for myself and for Megan. But I don't want to drive around."

"I've got an idea about that," he said, putting the van back in drive. "You have a cell phone?"

She nodded, then reached into her purse, pulling out a small phone in a black leather case. He told her the number to dial, and after she'd punched the numbers, she handed him the phone.

It rang twice. "Who the hell is it?" a scratchy voice asked. It was early—he'd awakened her. Of course, with Crystal, he could have called at noon and she'd still have been asleep.

"It's me," he said. He waited a moment, heard the click of a Bic and her quick inhalation as she took a drag on the day's first cigarette.

"I'm surprised you still remember the number."

"It's etched in my brain," he said, lowering his voice. "Like a certain rainy night."

She sighed into the phone. "What do you need, Jack?"

"A favor."

"I figured."

"I need to borrow the Caddy for a while. And put a van in your garage."

"You do, huh?"

"Yep." He glanced at Hailey. She was smiling at Megan, turned so he could see her face. Her color had come back, which he supposed was a good thing.

"How long do you need it for?"

"I'm not sure."

"I suppose it wouldn't do me any good to ask why?"

"Baby, you know me too well."

"Yeah. Too well." Then she paused. Exhaled. "Are you okay?"

"I'm great," he said, putting on his right signal. "Top of the world."

"My ass," she said.

"So I'll be there in fifteen, okay?"

"Why not."

"Thanks, Crystal. You're a doll."

She hung up without a goodbye. Crystal never liked goodbyes.

"We're borrowing a car?" Hailey asked.

He nodded. "A friend of mine has a couple she doesn't use. From a divorce settlement."

"I see."

"We'll put the van in her garage. No one will find it."

Hailey looked at him quizzically. "An ex-girlfriend?"

"Ex-wife."

"*Your* cars?"

He nodded.

"Oh," Hailey said, surprised.

He could see she wanted to ask him about it. How Crystal had gotten custody of the Caddy and the Mustang. But he didn't want to talk about it. The subject tended to make him a little grumpy.

They drove in silence for a while, until Hailey spotted a branch of her bank. Getting her money only took a minute, then he headed to Crystal's place in West University.

When he checked on Megan again, he saw she'd fallen asleep. Poor kid.

"Jack, after we get the car, I need to go to a store. A Wal-Mart or Target."

"Okay."

"And then…"

"Yeah?" He looked at her. She was nibbling on her lower lip. It was an unguarded move, innocent, childlike. And it did something to his insides. What, he wasn't sure. Was it protectiveness he felt? Guilt for getting her involved? Or was it just that he hadn't thought about the look of a woman's lower lip for a long long time?

"What are we going to do?" she asked finally.

"About what?"

"Everything."

He nodded. "We'll take it a step at a time," he said.

"I like that. I can deal with that. What's the first step?"

He smiled. "Getting the Cadillac."

She nodded. But she didn't nibble her lip again. He supposed it wasn't the kind of thing he could ask her to do. She'd probably wonder about him. He wouldn't blame her.

CRYSTAL CAME TO THE DOOR in her negligee. A diaphanous black floor-length gown that didn't hide any of her considerable charms. In fact, looking at that spectacular body made Hailey feel as though they weren't the same species, let alone the same gender. She thought about what she'd looked like last night wearing Jack's boxy pajamas. No wonder he hadn't given her a second glance. He had this to compare her to.

"I didn't know you were bringing the family," Crystal said, eyeing Hailey and the bundle of little girl and quilt in her arms.

"Surprise," Jack said. "The keys?"

"Why'd I ever divorce a charmer like you?" she asked, arching one perfect brow.

"Temporary insanity," he said, holding out his hand.

Crystal dropped a key ring into his palm. "The insanity was at the beginning, not the end."

"You're right." He shifted his leg, bracing his arm on his cane.

Crystal's gaze moved to his hip, then the cane. Her

brows came together as she frowned. "What's all this? You didn't tell me you needed a cane."

"It's temporary. No big deal."

"Jack," she said, looking up at him again, crossly, "you said it was nothing. That the bullet grazed you."

Hailey could see that Jack didn't want to talk about it. That it embarrassed him somehow that he'd been hurt. As if he should have been stronger than a bullet.

"Thanks for the car, kiddo," he said, ignoring her comment altogether. "I'll gas it up before I bring it back."

Crystal looked at Hailey. "Good luck, honey," she said. "You're going to need it."

Hailey wasn't sure if she was supposed to smile or not, so she did. But her thoughts stayed on the interaction between Jack and his ex while they transferred their belongings to the Cadillac.

She'd never met anyone like Jack before. Not even close. She couldn't imagine even one of the men in her life being so blasé about a woman like Crystal, let alone being shot. It was as if she'd gone through the looking glass, and everything familiar and easy had disappeared in the transition. Car chases, bad cops, women who looked like Rita Hayworth. Bizarre.

"You ready?" Jack asked as he put his cane into the backseat.

Hailey checked on Megan once more. She was safely belted in her car seat, awake now and sucking her thumb. "Let's go to McDonald's first," she said. "Megan needs to eat something."

"Right," he said, then put the car in gear and pulled out of the driveway.

Hailey looked at the house. Medium-size, brick, with a well-tended lawn. The house of a professor or a bank manager. How did Crystal end up there? Had Jack once lived there, too? She didn't think so. She couldn't picture him there. He wasn't the cozy neighborhood type. Not at all.

BY THE TIME they got settled in the house in Galveston, Jack's hip ached like a son of a bitch. It was late, almost four, and the last pill he'd taken was at breakfast, hours ago. Hailey was like a whirlwind, taking care that Megan was bathed, changed and fed, that the food they'd picked up at the grocery store was put away, and that the sheets on the beds were changed. He sat like a useless lump on a very comfortable leather chair, watching her accomplish her goals in an admirably efficient manner that appealed to his sense of order. He also just liked watching her.

She'd showered and changed along with Megan, and now wore a pair of black leggings and a sweatshirt from the University of Texas. He would have preferred a more revealing top, but at least her outfit afforded him a good look at her legs. And when she bent over, he silently applauded the way the material hugged her backside. It was a very good backside.

But after half an hour, he couldn't justify watching her any longer. He'd been thinking about the case, about the white car. It wasn't a police issue, of that he was certain. He hadn't gotten a look at the driver, thanks to that ski mask.

Who was he? How was he connected to the cop in Roy's apartment and the two cops in the unmarked car? One thing for certain, this was no small-time revenge hit. At least four people were involved, and that meant there was money and power somewhere. Another thing that had puzzled him all day was why the man in Hailey's apartment had asked about Megan. What would someone with money and power want with a four-year-old? Nothing. So it figured that whoever was behind this thought Megan had something important with her.

He'd gone through the contents of the pillowcase in his mind, and nothing seemed right. The picture? Maybe. He'd have to look at it more closely. The recipe? Was that some kind of code? There wasn't much else to suspect.

"Is your cell phone in your purse?" he asked, calling out to Hailey in the kitchen.

"Yes, right behind you. But there's a phone on the counter, next to the green vase."

"I don't want the number traced," he said as he pulled himself up, wondering if he should take his pill first and then call. His first step told him the answer to that was yes.

He grabbed the cell phone out of Hailey's purse, then went down the hall to the small bedroom that was going to be his for the next few days. It was nice, although a bit feminine for his taste. The queen-size bed had a canopy, which was a first for him, and the comforter on top was all flowery. The wallpaper had the same design, and there was a little vanity table in the corner with a bunch of perfume bottles, face stuff and hairbrushes.

Not that it mattered. He wasn't going to be here long. But it felt funny, especially after spending so much time in his apartment.

He opened his duffel and pulled out his bottle of pills. He shook it, grateful that he'd refilled his supply only two days ago. Then he opened it, took out two pills and swallowed them dry. Instead of putting the bottle back, he stuck it in his pocket.

The urge to lie down was strong, but he fought it, making his way back to the small living room. Hailey's parents had gone with a nautical theme, pictures of ships and lighthouses on the walls, mixed in with a whole array of family photos on the white bookcase. He'd seen one of Hailey when she was younger, eighteen or so. She'd been fresh and pretty back then, too. A real wholesome-looking girl. Someone he'd imagine in the 4H Club or home economics.

He dialed Frank O'Neill's number. It rang three times, four, and Jack was just about to hang up when Frank answered. "O'Neill."

"Hey, buddy."

"Jack! Where have you been? I've been trying to reach you all day."

"What for?"

"God, I've missed that savoir faire. I was calling because I've got four tickets to the Aeros for tomorrow night. Great seats. I figured we could call those sisters, you know, the ones from the bar?"

"I can't go," Jack said.

"It's not that much walking," Frank said. "I checked."

"It's not that. I'm away for a while. Taking a little vacation."

"From what? You don't do anything but sit on your ass all day as it is."

"I've missed your subtlety," Jack said, smiling. His ex-partner still cracked him up. Frank was like a tank, running over anything in his path, not delicate, not cautious, not polite. But he got the job done, and Jack trusted him with his life.

"You want subtle? Marry a geisha. You want the truth? Come to me."

"I am coming to you," Jack said, leaning against the wall so his full weight wasn't on his legs. "I need your help."

"What's up?"

"I need you to do some background checks—but on the quiet. Craig Faraday, first. Then a guy named Barry Strangis."

"Spell that last name."

Jack did. "One more," he said. "I want you to do some checking on a cop named Nichols."

"Brett Nichols?"

"Yeah. And while you're checking, see if there's any connection between Nichols and Strangis. Or Faraday."

Frank didn't say anything for a few moments, and Jack could picture him clearly as he sat at his desk, hunched over as usual, the end of his pencil in his mouth. He'd have his cups on his desk, plastic foam, at least five by now, each containing half a cup of cold coffee.

"Are you going to tell me what this is about?" he asked finally.

"Yeah. But later. Just do it and don't let anyone know you're doing it. Got that? No, wait. Talk to Bob Dorran. Get him to help."

"No one but Bob. Check. You sure you can't make it to the game?"

"I'm sure. I'll call you in a couple of days."

"Give me your number. I'll just call you when I'm finished."

"No. I'll call you."

"What is this?"

"You'll find out. I appreciate it, Franky."

"No sweat."

Jack hung up the phone. He looked over to see Hailey, standing just a few feet away. She'd been listening. "That was my partner."

"So you can trust him."

Jack nodded. "Yeah. I can trust him."

"But you still didn't give him the number here."

"The less he knows, the safer he is."

"And Bob Dorran?"

"A guy I went to the academy with. A real straight shooter."

"Do you think they'll find something?"

He shrugged. "We can do some searching ourselves," he said. "That is, if you're willing to help with that computer of yours."

She smiled, and he felt it in his chest. A pull the likes of which he'd never known before. He could have understood if he'd reacted with another part of his body, but this? This was something new. Something unsettling.

"You got it," she said. "If there's something to be found, we'll find it."

"Good enough."

"Dinner won't be ready for another hour or so. I've got Megan in my folks' bedroom watching cartoons, so she won't bother you if you want to take a nap."

He shook his head. "I think I'll take the shower I missed this morning." He rubbed his cheeks, the stubble rough on his hands. He must look like hell. Normally he wouldn't have cared. But he did. Today.

"There are fresh towels in the bathroom," she said. "In the long cabinet."

"Great."

"And, Jack?"

"Yes?"

"Thank you."

"For what?"

She sighed. "For helping."

He shrugged. "It's my job."

"Of course." She turned to go back into the kitchen, but stopped at the door. "You like meat loaf?"

"Love it."

"Good."

Then she smiled again and the pull came back. Stronger this time.

Peculiar. Damn peculiar.

Chapter Nine

Hailey scooted closer to Jack's chair as she waited for the Internet connection to complete. They were at the dining-room table, the dishes from their meal done two hours ago. Her laptop was in front of her, with Jack nearby so he could look at the small screen, too.

His arm and hers touched. His warmth seeped through his shirt and her bulky sweatshirt. The scent of him, clean and masculine, teased her, making her terribly aware of how large he was and how different. She wasn't at all sure why he should strike such a unique chord with her. He was just a man, after all. She'd certainly been this near other men. And yet...

Part of it was his attitude. She tried to imagine Steven asking for her help like this. They'd been together three years, and in all that time he'd never once asked for her advice. No, that wasn't true. He'd asked a few times, but only in front of her parents. Then he'd ignored anything she'd said. Even when she'd known more than he did, he'd never acknowledged it.

It had taken her a long time to come to trust herself after that. Sometimes even now she didn't. Especially when it came to men. At least she'd found her strength in the business world. That was something, wasn't it?

And Jack trusted her. She'd asked him to take a leap of faith and he had, no questions asked. That was something, too.

She focused again on the screen and put her fingers on the keyboard. She went right to the search engine she preferred. "Who first?"

"Let's do Barry Strangis," he said. "See what comes up."

She typed in the name and got a great many links, more than a hundred. But as she examined each brief synopsis of the connecting web sites, she saw that Barry Strangis was a far more common name than she could have imagined. Not one of the links seemed to have anything to do with the man she'd known as Roy Chandler. She looked at a few that were slight possibilities, but one was a television producer and the other was a gay man looking for a rendezvous with someone wearing spandex.

"Okay, then," Jack said. "Let's try Craig Faraday."

She went back to the start page and typed that name in. This time, there was a lot more information, most of it about the man they were researching. Newspaper articles, press releases, charities he was involved with. Faraday was well-known and had fingers in many pies. It would take a long time to go over all the data.

"You have a printer?"

She shook her head, but then she remembered. "Hold on." She hurried to her old bedroom, stopping briefly to peek in on Megan, who was sound asleep on the guest-room bed. She went to her closet and slid the door open. There, on the top shelf with hat boxes, an old pair of in-line skates and a broken kite, was her old printer. She'd brought it here about three years ago, but shortly after, she'd gotten a laser printer and had abandoned this ink-jet dinosaur. It might be slow and old, but it probably still worked.

She reached up and got it, blowing off a layer of dust as she went back to the living room. "Cross your fingers," she said. "I'm not sure it's going to work."

"If it doesn't, we'll go get one tomorrow."

"Hand me that dish towel, would you?" She put the printer on the table, then lifted the cable connector and plug out. She cleaned the machine as best she could and set it up for use.

When that was finished, she sat down and clicked on her home page, then she went to a link at the bottom that listed her price schedule. It was only one page and it would show them if the printer worked. She hit the right button and waited. It took a few minutes for things to warm up, but in the end, she had a nice clear black-and-white-printed page.

"How do you like that?" Jack said.

"I like it just fine. Now we hope I have enough paper and enough ink to print out all this stuff."

"We don't have to do it all tonight," he said. "Maybe a few things to read, and then we can make a trip to an office-supply store tomorrow. Hell, maybe we should do it all tomorrow. It's been a rough day.''

She stared at her screen, at the work represented. ''I agree. Tomorrow is soon enough. What I need is a glass of wine, a comfy place on the couch and some quiet.''

''I can leave if you want,'' he said, but she could see he was teasing her.

''I think there's a beer with your name on it in the fridge,'' she said, turning off the computer and unplugging everything.

''Ah, yes. A beer. The nectar of the gods.''

''Which gods would those be?'' She moved the equipment to a bench next to the dining-room wall.

''There's a whole lineup,'' he said, leaning back and stretching out his leg. He winced as he reached full extension. ''The god of football, the god of basketball…''

''And I suppose beer nuts are the food of the gods?''

He nodded. ''Beer nuts and pork rinds. They're very democratic, these gods.''

''I hope they're in league with the god of angioplasty or it could get pretty ugly.''

He laughed, and it was a great sound. Rich, easy. But then he moved his leg again and the laughter stopped.

''You know,'' she said. ''I haven't seen you do any of your exercises.''

He looked up sharply. ''What?''

''You said you do enough of the exercises the

physical therapist gave you. But I've yet to see you do any. You're supposed to do them every day.''

''We've been a little busy. Or hadn't you noticed?''

''We're not busy now.''

''Oh, no,'' he said. He stood up and started hobbling toward the big chair. ''I'm not in the mood for a torture session tonight.''

''Is it really that bad?'' She followed him into the living room. ''Honestly?''

He turned to face her, and she could see the answer on his face without his saying a word. It was bad. Really bad.

''Maybe I could help,'' she said. ''I know I hurt you last night, but that's because I wasn't sure where to move my hands. I've studied massage, you know. I used to work part-time at a spa.''

''I don't need a massage.''

''Of course you do. Everyone needs a massage.''

''Not me,'' he said, turning his back on her once more.

She shook her head, wondering how she could get him to relax enough around her to do the exercises. Although she wasn't a physical therapist, she knew enough to know that he wasn't ever going to walk without the cane if he didn't get down to some serious business.

Back in the kitchen she opened the bottle of white zinfandel she'd chilled and poured herself a glass. After a lovely sip, she got out his beer and headed back for round two. It occurred to her that he wasn't the kind of man who would run from pain, even though she knew stretching and manipulating his torn muscles would hurt like fire. But Jack? It didn't compute. He was too macho to let a little thing like pain get in his way. He wasn't doing his exercises for another reason. She had a couple of guesses, but she wasn't going to jump the gun. A little judicious probing wouldn't be amiss, however.

"Here," she said, holding out the beer bottle.

He took it eagerly. "Thanks."

"You're welcome," she said, watching him bring the bottle to his lips. He took a big swig of the brew, his Adam's apple moving up and down. It was nice that he'd shaved. She liked seeing all of him. But it also allowed her to see the lines bracketing his mouth, the wrinkles at the corners of his eyes. He was tired. More tired than she, and he deserved a rest.

They were going to be here for a few days at least. There would be time to talk about his injury. And his therapy. And who'd hurt him.

For tonight, though, it was going to be television and then bed.

SOMETHING POKED HIM in the cheek. He shifted, trying to get back to his dream, to Hailey rubbing his— another poke, harder this time. He opened his eyes.

There, inches from his face, stood Megan. She was in her pajamas, and for once she didn't have her doll tucked under her arm. She just stared at him, unmoving except for a blink every few seconds.

"Can I help you?" he asked, wondering what time

it was. It felt like dawn. Like he could have slept for another hour or five.

"Hailey says breakfast is almost ready."

"She does, does she?"

Megan nodded, which sent the curls on her head to bobbing. "She says you need to get up and into the shower."

"I see."

"And she says you polished off a lot of beer last night, so it's no wonder you feel like heck in the morning."

"Like heck?"

Megan nodded. "It's not a bad word. I asked."

"You did, huh?"

"Your breath smells bad."

He smiled. "I'd better go brush my teeth then, huh?"

She nodded again.

"You go on and help Hailey," he said. "I'll be out soon."

"Okay."

He watched her walk to his bedroom door, amazed at how little she was. It occurred to him that she was an actual person. He'd never really considered that before. Kids were just a group he lumped together, like puppies or kittens. Then, when they hit about fourteen, he tended to think of them as juvenile delinquents. It wasn't until they reached drinking age that they became people.

But maybe his vision had been a little narrow. Maybe.

He threw off his covers and pushed himself up,

his hip reminding him what a damn fool he was. He should do his exercises, Hailey was right about that. But he didn't want to. Especially not around her.

After he swallowed his first pill of the day, he headed for the shower. As he walked down the hallway, he heard Hailey laugh, and it made him want to see her, want to know what she was laughing about. Instead, he went into the bathroom and locked the door behind him.

Dreaming about her was one thing, but wanting her during the day was another. There was no way anything could happen. Even if she'd let him, he couldn't do much to satisfy her. The thought of that particular humiliation was more than he could bear. It wasn't that he couldn't function—that part worked just fine. It was the rest of his body that was uncooperative. Ungainly. Ugly.

He wanted to talk to whomever was in charge. The jokester who had put him in such close proximity to a woman whose smile made him ache, when he couldn't do a damn thing about it. Ha-ha. Very amusing.

He turned on the shower, then took off his pajamas. The scar on his hip mocked him. A deep, red gash that made him wince just looking at it. She'd be repulsed. He wouldn't blame her.

THE STACK OF PAGES between them was daunting. Faraday was a public figure, and it seemed to Jack that every move the man made was documented in one form or another. It would take them all day to get through this pile, and it wasn't likely they'd turn up anything at all about Barry Strangis.

But there wasn't anything else to do. O'Neill and Dorran were doing the real legwork—the work Jack would have done if he'd been whole. What was left was this. Reading. Thinking too damn much.

He looked at Hailey, sitting on the other end of the couch. Her legs were curled under her, and he could see her pink socks. She had on navy leggings and a navy sweater, but her socks were pink. He couldn't figure out why. Did she not have any other color? Did she have a thing for pink socks?

"Getting a lot of reading done there, Jack?"

He blinked and saw her smiling at him. "Just thinking."

"Uh-huh."

He moved his gaze back to the printout in his lap. It was an article about zoning in Chicago. Dull as dishwater and full of political crap, it didn't tell him anything about Faraday or Strangis. But he kept on reading just in case.

He'd gotten to page three when the sound of Megan's cartoons edged in. High squeals, boings, violins. And then the unmistakable beep-beep of the Road Runner. He used to like those cartoons. Wile E. Coyote, Acme Rentals. Jeez.

Of course, Megan herself wasn't even watching the cartoons. She was on the floor, on her quilt, talking to herself, as he'd seen her do several times. He wondered what was in her head. What all those eyes and bumblebees and houses and cats on the quilt were about. Why some squares were red and why they weren't symmetrical. He was sure any woman would make sense of the pattern immediately, but to him it just looked like a big jumble. The kid sure liked it, though.

Then his gaze moved again to Hailey. He couldn't help it. God, she was so different from Crystal. Polar opposites. Crystal was a real firecracker, one with a damn-short fuse. Impatient, unpredictable, moody. And just about as selfish as he was. But she was great in the sack. Now, he'd wager Hailey was great in the sack, too, but not the same at all. She was patient and innocent and not so sure of herself. But he bet she was passionate. A slow candle that would burn for a long long time.

"What's that smile for?"

Shoot. She'd caught him. "Nothing," he said as he tried to find his place in the article.

"Nothing my behind. That was a very telling smile, mister."

He shook his head. "I was just thinking about Crystal."

"Oh," she said, but her voice sounded strange. He looked at her. Her smile had disappeared and she'd stiffened her shoulders. There was a hint of a blush on her cheeks. It was confusing. All he'd said was…

Could Hailey be jealous? No. No, that was nuts. Crazy. She didn't think of him that way. It wasn't possible. But then he saw her fingers ripping little pieces off the page she was reading.

"I was thinking," he said, "about how my marriage was a joke."

Hailey's head snapped back. "What?"

"Nothing. Just…I don't know. We were wrong for each other is all. From the start."

"Why did you marry her, then?"

"We were drunk, in Las Vegas, and we'd just won a bundle at the craps table. It seemed like a great idea."

Her smile was coming back. A little lift on the corners, not a big grin. But it was something. Maybe she *had* been jealous. How about that?

"How long were you two together?"

"It felt like twenty years. But it was only two. A little less than that, actually."

"I'm sorry," she said.

"Don't be. We deserved each other."

"How did she end up with the cars?"

He laughed, although it wasn't at all funny. "It was my penance."

"For what?"

"For believing in love."

She didn't say anything. She looked at him differently, though. As if what he'd said confirmed something she'd guessed—probably that he was a jackass. He put the article he was reading on the end table and picked up the next one in the stack. This one was about Faraday's work with the End Hunger Project. He read the first line, then had to read it again when it didn't register. What he needed was a beer. He looked at his watch. It was almost noon. Late enough. Hell, if he was at home, he'd have had a beer for breakfast.

He got up, struggling as usual with the cane and his hip, cursing as usual under his breath. As he moved toward the kitchen, he thought about something to eat with his beer. Potato chips, maybe. Maybe not. He opened the fridge door, but he didn't see the beer. He bent down, looking behind the milk carton and the orange juice. Nothing. Not a single beer. He hadn't finished off *all* the beer last night. There were a couple of six-packs in there yesterday. He'd put them there himself. "Hailey?"

"Yes?" She answered too quickly. Too sweetly.

"Do you know where the beer is?"

"Yes," she said again in that same singsong voice.

"Would you like to tell me?" He shut the door and turned to look at her. He could see into the living room from the kitchen. She was standing, smiling enigmatically.

"Hey, what's going on?" he asked.

"I'll be right back," she said. Then she walked out of the living room and went down the hall to her bedroom.

She was up to something, but what? Maybe it was religious. He wasn't sure what she was, but maybe she didn't believe in liquor. No, she'd had wine last night.

She came back into the living room, holding a big brown plastic rolled-up mat in her arms, which she proceeded to unroll on the carpet. An exercise mat. Somehow he knew it wasn't for her own use. "What's that for?"

"Exercising."

"What does that have to do with my beer?"

She took in a deep breath and let it out in a whoosh. "Pretty much everything."

Growing angrier by the second, he headed for her, completely flabbergasted at her audacity. "You'd better be joking," he said, letting her know with his voice, with his eyes, that *he* wasn't.

She took a step back, then stopped. Straightened her shoulders. Pursed her lips. "I'm not joking at all."

"Hailey, this isn't funny."

"That's right. It isn't. Those muscles and tendons will never work right again until you teach them how. So here's the deal. You exercise, you can have your beer."

"Not a chance."

"Okay, then. Have it your way."

"Hailey, where's the beer?"

"I'm not telling you."

"What the hell are you doing? I'm not some kid you can treat this way."

"You're not? You're certainly acting like one."

"I'm warning you," he said, his blood pounding in his temples. "Knock it off."

"No," she said. Just like that. No.

"What do you mean, no?"

"No. What part of no don't you understand?"

He moved closer. Close enough to see that she was shaking. For all her bravado, she was scared out of her wits. But she didn't back down. Not an inch. "This is unbelievable," he growled.

Her eyes widened and she shook her head in disbelief. "I know!"

"What?"

"It *is* unbelievable. I never do things like this. Usually I'm a pussycat."

"Don't change for my benefit."

"I am, though. Changing for your benefit. I'm not sure why, but that doesn't seem to matter. I...I'm not going to budge."

Now he was completely confused. She was scared and brave. Bewildered and adamant. Outrageous and completely certain. "You know, all I have to do is get in the car and go buy some more."

She nodded. "I know. It would seem that way."

He closed his eyes for a moment and counted silently to ten. When he opened them again, he still wanted to strangle her. "You've hidden the keys?"

She gave him an apologetic smile as she nodded, and her blond hair bobbed, just like Megan's always did. But that was off the subject. Right now he needed to be angry. And he needed her to back off.

"Look, I understand that you think I should do the damn exercises. And I will. Just not now."

"When?"

"I don't know. When I'm good and ready!"

"Then I'll give you the beer when *I'm* good and ready!"

"You can't do that!"

"But I am!"

"I... You..." He shut his mouth, because he couldn't think of what to say. Nobody talked to him that way and lived to tell it. Nobody. He ought to...

Kiss her. Take her in his arms and kiss her the

way she deserved to be kissed. Kiss her till her knees grew weak and her heart pounded.

He took a step and then another. And then he saw it in her eyes. She knew what he was going to do. She gasped, a quiet quick little intake of breath that made her mouth open into a perfect O.

He took the last step and leaned forward.

Chapter Ten

Hailey saw him lean forward, the intensity of his emotions all there in his eyes. Heat, anger and something she couldn't identify. Something so strong she became instantly frightened and exhilarated. She felt as though her heart stopped beating, her lungs stopped breathing.

His lips touched hers and she closed her eyes, abandoning herself to sensation. His arm went around her back, and he brought her closer, branding her with his kiss. Hot, moist, thrilling. She found herself kissing him back, wanting more and more. Snaking her hand around his neck to hold him good and steady while she teased and was teased in return.

Giddy and trembling, she felt him explore her more deeply. Tasting him so intimately, his scent all around her, and the feel of his hand on her back was perfect. The kiss was something entirely different, entirely wonderful. Steven had kissed her with his mouth so wide open she felt as though she would fall in. But Jack, he knew the exact amount of pressure, when to ease up, when to nip her lower lip.

This wasn't like any kissing she'd known before. This was heaven. And all she wanted was more.

He shifted again, moving closer, so his body and hers touched from lips to knees. And then he moved his hand down her back, his touch making her quiver.

He pulled his head back, breaking the kiss, forcing her to gaze into his eyes. To see the desire there. The need. And when she couldn't stand it another second, he leaned forward to kiss her again, only something went wrong. He stumbled forward, knocking into her, grabbing the back of her sweatshirt with his free hand. She tried to hold him steady, but her foot got caught on the exercise mat, and she almost fell. In the nick of time he moved his cane and got his balance.

She started to laugh until she saw his face. He looked utterly humiliated. His cheeks and forehead red with shame, his gaze casting about for a safe place to look. His whole body rigid with mortification.

"Jack?"

He gripped the head of his cane with both hands, and turned away from her.

"It's okay. It was just a little slip, that's all."

He didn't answer her, and she knew she'd better shut up, even though she wasn't at all clear why such a little thing should bother him so much. It was enough to know it did.

She watched him walk away, his limp more pronounced than ever with his posture so stiff and unyielding. All the electricity that had swirled inside her just a moment ago drained away. The perfect kiss had turned into the perfect tragedy, and she wasn't sure why or what she could do about it. Her instinct was to help him, but in this case, in his case, she knew that leaving him alone was the best thing she could do.

Such a shame. Such a damn shame. He'd touched something very deep inside her with that kiss. Something she'd never felt before. As if he'd lit a pilot light, destined to burn for a long time. Waiting to be stoked into a blaze. A blaze that would never come.

He wasn't going to kiss her again. She felt sure of that. And she didn't know if she had the guts to initiate it herself. Probably not. She'd never been brazen like that. It had shocked her to pieces that she'd hidden his beer. That she'd stood up to his anger. There was no way she could stand up to his shame.

Sighing, she went into the kitchen, dragging a chair behind her. She climbed on the chair so she could reach the cupboard above the refrigerator and get his beer. All of it. And then she slowly climbed down. The game was over before it had really begun. Just her luck.

She put the bottles in the fridge, wishing she was smarter. Some women knew instinctively how to handle situations like this, she was sure of it.

As she returned the chair to the dining-room table, she saw Jack come back to the living room. He didn't look at her. Not even a glance. Instead, he went over to the exercise mat.

For a moment she thought he was going to kick it. To send it flying against the far wall. But that was not what happened.

He leaned to his right, very heavily on his cane. It took her a minute to realize he was sitting down. She had to close her eyes, though. The simple act of kneeling was something monumental. A struggle of balance and fortitude.

She never should have pushed him. She had no business sticking her nose where it didn't belong. When she heard his stifled groan, she cringed.

Finally she opened her eyes again. Jack had made it down all the way. He sat, looking uncomfortable and awkward, on the mat, legs straight out in front of him.

He bent forward. He didn't get very far. His hands hovered over his legs, just below his knees, for a count of two and then he straightened for another count of two. Repeating the motion, he got a tiny bit farther. But he was doing it too quickly. Each move should have lasted for the count of ten.

She wondered if she should go to him. Would offering her assistance make things worse? Would he give up entirely?

Oh, what the hell. Things couldn't get much worse. The least she could do was help him make the exercises count.

He looked up at her as she slowly approached him, but it was just a quick glare. Clearly she wasn't very high on his hit parade at the moment. She pasted a smile on and went to kneel next to him on the floor.

Jack just kept bending forward and straightening. One-two, one-two. Hailey put her hand gently on his back.

"I don't need your help," he said, his voice as cold as the ice in the fridge.

"Well, yeah, you do," she said as gently as possible. "You're going too fast. You need to count to five each time."

He didn't move for a long while. Way past five. She didn't remove her hand. She simply waited. Then he inhaled and stretched forward, and she counted to herself. One, two, three, four, five. He sat straight again, exhaling, and rested for another count of five.

"Okay," she said, "that's good. But this time, exhale as you make the stretch."

She listened to his breath, felt his back expand and contract as he bent again. "Good, that's good," she whispered. Ten more times, he did the same exercise, and each time he did it perfectly. She counted with him, exhaled when he did, coaxed him past his comfort zone. Then she moved down to the base of the mat, where his feet were. He had his boots on, the only footwear he'd taken with him. She pulled them off one at a time. "Lay back," she said.

He did. Without complaint and without any conversation, either. It wasn't right. But she didn't know how to change things.

Lifting his right foot, she brought it up, close to her chest. "Exhale," she said, and then she pushed forward, bending his leg and pushing it back toward his chest.

He grimaced with the pain of the movement and stopped breathing altogether. She held his leg in the farthest extension for five, then slowly, to the count of ten, straightened it. "Remember, breath out on the effort."

Again she moved his leg, stretching damaged and weak muscles where they didn't want to go. Each time, he got better at breathing and it appeared to hurt him less. Until she moved to the other leg, when the pain cycle repeated itself. By the time they were through, he had a sheen of sweat on his brow, and his arms and legs were more mush than muscle.

"Roll over," she said.

He quirked his head. "I don't have any exercises on my stomach."

"I know. Just do it."

He did, his body so uncooperative that he rolled off the mat completely, then had to inch his way back. She stood up and went into her bedroom. Her parents' bedroom, actually, but where she was sleeping. She got one of the feather pillows and a bottle of lotion and then returned to him. Before she sat again, she peeked at Megan. She expected to find her asleep, she'd been so quiet. But she wasn't. Her eyelids drooped and her thumb-sucking lacked enthusiasm, but her gaze was focused on *Animaniacs*. Hailey went over and gave her a little kiss on the top of the head. Megan looked up briefly, but the TV called her immediately back.

When Hailey turned to Jack, she watched his back rise and fall rapidly. He was winded. Struggling to calm down. The workout had been just that. The guy needed a break and she intended to give it to him.

She got down again, only this time, she straddled

his butt, making sure not to rest her weight on him. "Take off your shirt," she said.

"I don't want a massage," he said.

"Sure you do."

"Hailey, I—"

She put her hand on his back again, stilling his protest. "It'll help, big guy. Trust me."

He grabbed the bottom of his polo shirt and tugged it up. She put the pillow under his head and then she pulled the shirt off the rest of the way.

"Now, concentrate on breathing," she said softly, using her massage voice. The one that put most of her clients to sleep. "Go deep with each breath, and picture healing light going to your hips and legs."

She squirted some lotion into her hands and rubbed them together to make them warm. Then she leaned forward and began the massage.

Of course, he tensed immediately. She'd been expecting that. Especially after the kiss. But she didn't ease up, not an iota. All her techniques came back to her, even though she hadn't used this particular skill in years. Long slow strokes up and down the length of his back, warming his smooth skin. He felt so good under her hands, so firm, so muscular. Her goal was to ease the knots in his muscles, relax the tension centered in his shoulder blades. Get his circulation pumping so his body could heal itself.

Ten minutes into it, he finally relaxed. She had the feeling if he hadn't been so tired, he would have fought her until the cows came home, but she had the advantage. He simply didn't have the energy to keep from feeling good.

She moved her hands down, to the small of his back, and used her knuckles to knead his flesh. Deeper and deeper, using her body weight as a lever. He moaned, but it was a good moan. She could tell the difference. Then she went back up to his shoulders, and she rubbed and stroked and used every trick in her arsenal to give him pleasure and relief.

She became mesmerized by her own movements, by the sheen of his skin beneath her. Her breathing slowed as she rode him, touching his bottom lightly with each forward push, then rising with the backward pull. It became a dance, a sensuous tango of bare skin and lotion.

Her thoughts took a turn, first to the memory of his lips on hers and then way beyond. If he was on his back. Naked. And she was naked, riding him like this, rubbing him like this. Feeling him inside her as she moved her hips up and down.

She closed her eyes, swept away on a tide of eroticism. Heat swirled at the junction of her thighs as the urge to find a relief of her own built and built.

He moaned again and she smiled, knowing she had still another trick up her sleeve. If Megan wasn't there, if they were alone…

"Hailey." His hand on hers. Stilling her. "Hailey."

"What's wrong?" she asked, afraid she'd hurt him without realizing it.

"Stop now. Stop."

"But—"

"For God's sake, woman, you're killing me."

She pulled her hands away, not understanding how

she could be hurting him. And then it dawned on her that she wasn't hurting him physically. At least not his old wounds. But somehow the tide that had carried her away had swept him up, too.

She stood up and walked into the kitchen, embarrassed that she'd been so transparent, so blatant. That her thoughts had become so X-rated. It had never happened to her before, not even when she'd massaged that gorgeous Rocket guard.

Jack still lay on his stomach, his head cradled in his arms now, instead of the pillow. She got one of his beers from the fridge and opened it. He didn't move at all as she came back to stand next to him. "Hey," she said.

He grunted.

"I have something for you."

He opened one eye and peeked up at her. When he saw the beer, he gave her a grudging grin. "I didn't do it for the beer."

"Now, Jack. Once I've put lotion on a person's back, it means we have to tell the truth to each other."

"I am," he said, pushing himself up to a sitting position and taking the beer from her. He took a big swig, then made a face. "This isn't cold."

"You want me to get you some ice?"

"Ice? In beer?"

"Sorry," she said, "I didn't realize I was suggesting blasphemy."

"Ice in beer," he said again, shaking his head as if she'd just suggested they walk on the moon.

"So why'd you do it, big guy? If not for the beer?"

His face grew serious as he looked up at her. "You know."

She thought she might, but she wasn't sure. Was it the kiss? The promise of more?

"I did it because you asked me to."

The fluttery sensation came back to her stomach, and she felt her cheeks heat with embarrassed pleasure. "That's nice. We'll do it again tomorrow. Only this time, I won't hide your beer."

He took in a deep breath, and she could see he was thinking how much he didn't want to agree. But he nodded. Then he did a surprising thing—he held out his free hand. "Give a cripple a boost?" he joked.

"That's not funny," she said, taking his hand and pulling him to his feet.

"Right," he said. "I forgot. I'm differently-abled. Or has it changed to something more politically correct since I last looked?"

"I don't see you as a label, Jack. Not even when I'm teasing."

"No? How do you see me?"

He was so close to her she could see the tiny flecks of gold in his dark brown eyes. She could smell the scent of the lotion on his back and shoulders. Her gaze dropped to his chest, not so much to check him out as to break away from his intense questioning gaze. It proved to be an extraordinary distraction. He was a beautifully built man. Just the perfect amount of muscle and dark hair. Next time she must remember to start her massage before he rolled over.

"Is it that bad?"

She looked up, realizing she hadn't answered his question. "How do I see you?" she repeated, thinking about her answer. "Enigmatic. Strong. Smart. And wounded."

"That last thing was kind of obvious, no?"

She shook her head. "I'm not talking about the bullet."

His hand still rested on her arm. He moved it to her face, a gentle caress with his warm palm across her cheek. "Don't do that," he said softly. "I know you want to fix the world, but some things are so broken they can't ever be fixed."

"You'd be surprised," she whispered, held fast by his gaze, by the world of hurt she saw there.

"No, I wouldn't. I know a few things, Hailey. Not many, but a few. And I know that if and when I can walk normally again, I won't ever be the man you think I can be."

"How do you know what I think?"

His lips curled into a smile. "It's all right there, kiddo. Right on that pretty face. All the fairy tales are in your eyes, and there's not a thing you can do to hide it."

She turned away, but his hand captured her chin. Forcing her once more to look at him.

"Someday you'll find the right guy," he said. "The lucky bastard."

She took his hand away. "Now who's being naive?"

He pointed to his cane and she got it for him. After another swig from his warm beer, he leaned away so he wasn't touching her anymore. A swirl of disappointment hit, surprising her in its acuteness. She'd liked being there for him to lean on. She'd liked it very much.

"Look who's come up from the land of *Merry Melodies*," Jack said, pointing with his chin.

She looked over to see Megan and Tottie, standing up on the leather chair, peeking over the top. "Hi there."

"Tottie's hungry," Megan said.

"Hmm. How about you? Are you hungry, too?" Megan nodded.

"Any requests?"

Megan nodded again.

"What?"

"I want a hot dog."

"Now that sounds delicious," Hailey said, crossing to the chair. She kissed Megan on the forehead. "One hot dog, coming right up."

"Can Tottie have a beer?"

Hailey laughed. "A beer? She's too young to drink a beer."

Megan sighed, accepting defeat graciously. But she didn't laugh. She hadn't laughed at all during her cartoon marathon. Or when Hailey had teased her this morning. The little girl and the big strong man had more in common than they knew. Both of them had lost something precious. Both of them needed so much to believe in something again. To see a future that wasn't all shadows and fog.

She didn't think she could help the man, but there was no way she was going to give up on the little girl. "Would you like to help me make lunch?"

Megan nodded, then turned to climb down from the chair. She walked over to Jack and looked up at him. "Are you going to help, too?"

He appeared puzzled and not just a little panicked. "Uh, sure."

She held out her hand. Her tiny hand. He set his beer bottle on the end table, then took that little hand in his, swallowing it whole. Megan led him to the kitchen.

Hailey had to blink awfully fast to stop the tears that threatened. She was such a sentimental fool.

Chapter Eleven

Hailey glanced at Jack, who was on the phone. He had a soda instead of a beer and that was a good sign. She turned back to Megan and the same game they always played. Actually, in the past few months, Megan had been more interested in other things, but since her father's death, all she wanted was Tottie and the quilt.

The game was more of a story than anything else, with Hailey asking questions about the pictures. Who was Mrs. Bee? Where did the little girl walk? What was this letter, that number? It was a very clever approach to teaching, and it seemed such a comfort to Megan that Hailey didn't mind repeating the stories time and time again. Although it occurred to Hailey that it was a rather sad story. The little girl was alone, with no one to help her. Maybe that was why Megan was so attached to it. Because she was alone, too.

It was hard to concentrate on the little one when she wanted to hear Jack's conversation. It was his friend, Bob Dorran, and she felt sure he'd uncovered something about Roy. She shouldn't call him that. His name was Barry. Barry Strangis. Which brought up the question of why he'd changed his name. Lots of people had troubled pasts without going to such extreme measures. Why had he gotten himself into so much trouble that he'd left his only daughter an orphan?

She wondered if there'd been a birth certificate in the apartment. If whoever had trashed the place had found it, and if the name on it was Megan Chandler or Megan Strangis. If it was Strangis, then the bad guys knew about Roy's alias. She was sure that was significant, but she didn't know why.

"Hailey?" Megan said, tugging on her sweatshirt.

"Yes, honey?"

"Look." Megan pointed to the picture of a kitten. "She's Molly and she purrs at night. And Daddy says that when I'm old enough to take care of her, we can get a real kitty." Megan's lips pursed and her little eyebrows came down. "I s'pose I can't get a kitty now."

"Why not?"

"'Cause I'll never be old enough to take care of her."

"What do you mean, sweetie?" Hailey asked, moving closer, her attention completely focused on Megan.

"'Cause I'm going to go to heaven soon."

Hailey picked Megan up and put her on her lap. She wrapped her arms around her and held her tight. "You're not going to heaven soon, my love. No one's going to hurt you. You're going to live with me. And I know that's not as good as living with your mommy and daddy, but it won't be too bad. You'll see. We'll be very very good friends. And when we go back home, we'll pick out a kitty all for you.''

''Will I live in your 'partment?''

''Yes, for a while. Until we move to *our* apartment. One where you can have your own bedroom.''

''Will Jack live with us, too?''

''No, hon, he won't. He's here just for a little while.''

''Why?''

''Because he lives in his own apartment. See, Jack is a policeman. Do you know what a policeman is? He helps people who've been hurt. It's a very hard job.''

Megan seemed to consider this for a long moment. She ran her foot over the edge of a red quilt square, tracing the line up and over. Hailey was amazed at how small that sneaker was. No longer than the width of her palm. Such a tiny thing to hold such huge pain.

''Hailey?''

''Yes?''

''How come Jack walks funny?''

''Because he was hurt. That's why we were doing exercises today. To help him feel better.''

''I don't...I mean, you said Jack helps people who get hurt.''

''That's right.''

''So then you help Jack?''

''We can both help Jack,'' Hailey said.

Megan looked at her. "I can't help. I'm only four."

Behind them Jack cleared his throat. Hailey turned to look, surprised he wasn't still on the phone, then turned her attention back to Megan. "Tell you what," she said. "Why don't you go sit with Jack and ask him how you can help. I'll go in the kitchen and fix us all a bowl of ice cream. How does that sound?"

"Good," Megan said. She climbed out of Hailey's lap dragging Tottie behind her. She headed for Jack, who'd moved to sit on the couch.

It was hard for Hailey not to laugh when she got a load of Jack's reaction to her little plan. He looked as though she'd just condemned him to a fate worse than death. Actually, he needed a dose of Megan. Get his mind off his own problems.

Megan got to the couch and climbed up, which was no minor feat for someone smaller than the sofa cushion. Then she scooted over until she was sitting right next to him, her legs not even reaching the edge of the seat.

He looked down, opened his mouth and shut it again.

She looked up and wiped a stray curl from her forehead.

The standoff lasted a good minute.

Finally Jack said, "Hey."

Megan shifted Tottie on her lap. "Hey."

"So, uh, you and Hailey were, uh, talking?"

She nodded. "She said you need help."

"She did?" He glanced at Hailey just long enough

to give her the evil eye, then turned back to Megan. "She's right. I do."

"She said I should help you."

"I see. Did she say how?"

Megan shook her head. "She said you'd tell me."

"Great."

"I could carry something."

"Huh?"

"I could carry something. When you walk around. Then you wouldn't have to carry it."

He nodded. "You know, I think that's exactly what I need. Someone to carry something."

She sighed, a big old chest-heaver, as if solving this problem had relieved a heavy burden. "I usually carry Tottie."

"I know."

"But I don't have to all the time."

"That's nice of you," Jack said.

"I know."

He smiled and leaned closer to Megan. "Is Hailey still watching us?" he whispered, loud enough for Hailey to hear.

Megan nodded.

"Isn't she supposed to be getting us ice cream?"

Megan nodded again.

"All right!" Hailey said, hating to move away. Watching the two of them stirred something deep inside her. Of course, her maternal instincts were in high gear around Megan, but it was watching Jack that gave her this lump in her throat. He was so big he could have picked Megan up with one hand, like a football. And yet he was so tender with her. Maybe out of fear, or maybe because of his good heart. Probably a combination of both.

He didn't know it, but he'd make a wonderful father. For a boy or a girl. She could see the signs, and it made her wish for a crazy second that Jack could come back and live in her apartment. Megan needed a father. Of course, she'd be okay without one, but it wasn't the best situation for a child.

She got the ice cream out of the freezer and three bowls from a cupboard. As she scooped out the Rocky Road, she thought about what had happened this afternoon. His lips on hers. Her hands on his back. The sensation of his skin, the feel of his muscled flesh, hadn't left her. Not through dinner or dishwashing or Megan's bath or storytime. It hovered inside her. Sense memories. She'd be in the middle of a sentence and she'd suddenly find her hand tingling. Or smell his unique scent, even when he was across the room.

She was attracted to him. Big time. Like she'd never been attracted to anyone before. Ever since she'd seen Megan on his lap back at his place. That had been the moment it changed. But so what? Nothing was going to come of it. Despite the kiss. Despite the electricity between them.

He'd said so.

But why didn't the butterflies stop? Why did she want to keep looking at him? To catalog each feature, memorize every facet of his face?

Just her luck. Which, as far as men went, was lousy times ten. She'd stayed with Steven too long, even though she'd known he wasn't a nice man. But the fear of being alone had been stronger than the reality of staying with him. For a while at least. Finally it had been unbearable.

She hadn't escaped unscathed, though. And that was her biggest fear. That she would repeat her mistakes. That her desire to be close to someone would lead her down the wrong path. That she *was* as weak as Steven had believed her to be.

What if Jack was like Steven? Their styles were completely different and Jack was much nicer—on the surface. He was grouchier than Steven, but the way he tried so hard with Megan…

What was he like deep down? Seeing Crystal was a clue. He certainly hadn't made that work. And his apartment! That was a big hint, wasn't it? Nothing but the barest necessities. More a prison than a home.

She picked up the bowls and took them in to the dining room. Then she looked at the couch. Jack held Tottie up in front of him. Why, she couldn't fathom. He lowered the doll and handed her back to Megan. She couldn't hear his words, but Megan's smile told her he'd done something good.

Just seeing that filled her with warmth. Made her want to touch him. To give him the home he deserved. *Hailey McCabe.* She tried out the name, weighed the syllables and cadence. It would fit her.

She sighed. In her dreams. This wasn't a love story and he wasn't her destiny. Circumstances had brought them together, not desire. She'd seen too many movies, that was all. Read too many romance novels.

"Come and get it," she said, as she put the bowls on the table.

JACK TOOK HIS PILL and waited for Hailey to finish putting Megan to bed. The exercising had him aching in all the old familiar places and a few more besides. But she was right. He did need to try, even though he knew the outcome. Sure, he'd be able to lose the cane in time. But he'd limp forever. He'd have his scars forever. He'd never again be Jack McCabe. Not the Jack McCabe he wanted to be.

The problem, as he saw it, was that while they were hiding out here, Hailey was going to work with him. Touch him. He'd already decided she wasn't going to give him another massage. Not a chance. While her capable hands had been amazing for his muscles, the rest of him had gone crazy. He'd never really relaxed. He couldn't. Not while his libido, which had been dormant for so long, kicked into high gear.

God, he wanted her. Wanted her like he had never wanted anyone before. Undoubtedly that was simply because he'd been a monk for so many months. A man feels strange things after a month. After several? He couldn't be held responsible.

The strangest symptom of all was the desire he felt to know her. Not just in the biblical sense. He was curious about her life. About where she'd come from and what she hoped for. *That* had never happened before. It confused him and he didn't like it. Better they keep things impersonal. Once this mess was over, they'd both go back to their real lives. Of course, there was the fact that he didn't have a life, but that shouldn't enter into the equation.

It would have been so much easier if he was whole. If he was actively working to solve the case and focused on the one thing he could count on. His job. It had been his whole world for so long that all he was left with now was empty space. Hailey had just walked in at the wrong time, that was all.

He was no psychology expert, but he recognized the signs that his feelings for her were transference. He couldn't have his work, so he wanted to have the woman. A textbook case. And a no-win situation.

He heard her footsteps. He felt embarrassed, as if she'd be able to tell what he'd been thinking about. If that wasn't proof he'd gone over the edge, he didn't know what was.

"She's out," Hailey said as she joined him on the couch. She tipped her head from side to side, as if working out kinks in her neck.

"You okay?"

She nodded. "I'm fine. I just wish I could do more for Megan. I don't like it that her sleeping patterns are so irregular."

"She's been through a lot. Give her time."

"I'd feel better if we were home."

"Yeah," he said, achingly aware of how close Hailey was. She hadn't sat at the other end of the couch. Instead, she was just inches away. Close enough that he could easily touch her thigh.

She'd be something, without that baggy shirt. Without any clothes at all. The woman had curves where curves ought to be. She wasn't too big, but, thank God, she wasn't emaciated like many women he knew. He could just imagine the feel of her in his arms—

"So," she said, breaking into his thoughts, "what did your friend say?"

"Friend?"

She gave him a questioning smile. "Bob Dorran."

"Oh, yeah. Okay." He shifted a bit on the couch to hide his uneasiness. "Bob confirmed something I'd heard about. Faraday, for all his public show of charity, is connected."

She blinked. "To what?"

"Organized crime."

"The Mafia?"

He nodded. "There's no proof, but Frank knows people. If he says Faraday's connected, then he is."

"So what does that mean?"

"I don't know. But I think it's interesting that he's here."

"In Houston, you mean?"

"Yep. Setting up new offices. He's been there for about a month. Spreading the wealth around. The stock in UTI has gone through the roof. Evidently he's expanding into offshore oil drilling, and he's working the environmentalists."

"I still don't see what it has to do with Roy."

Jack shook his head, wishing he could tell her more. "I'm going to call Mr. Faraday tomorrow. If he's mixed up with the mob, then it stands to reason that Roy was, too. I'm thinking Roy crossed someone he shouldn't have. Maybe borrowed some money he couldn't pay back."

"They really do kill people for that?"

He nodded. "You bet."

"But didn't you say you saw an unmarked police car at the scene?"

"Yeah, I did."

"So which is it? The Mafia or the police?"

He shrugged. "For all I know, it's both."

"Oh, my."

"That's one way of putting it."

She frowned and studied a spot on the carpet. "Let's assume that's it. That somehow some cops are involved with the Mafia and that Roy got himself into enough hot water to get himself killed. It's clear that the murder didn't fix the problem. If it had, the apartment wouldn't have been searched, and Nichols wouldn't have been there."

"Right. So Roy had something they wanted. Money. Or information."

"Which doesn't explain why the man in my apartment wanted to know where Megan was."

"Unless they think she knows where the stuff is."

Hailey looked at him. "She's four. What could she possibly know?"

"I don't think it's the girl they're after. But something they think she has."

"The pillowcase," Hailey said, nodding.

"I don't think so," Jack said. "We've looked at everything in there so many times."

"The recipe? Could it be a code?"

"I don't know. If it is, it's way beyond me." He shook his head. "I don't think it's the contents of the pillowcase. I think it's something else. Something we're missing."

"Like what?"

Jack shrugged.

"We'll go over everything again tomorrow," she said. "When we've both had a good night's sleep. Right now I couldn't figure out two plus two."

"What's wrong?"

"Nothing. Except that I'm so tired I can't think straight."

"You didn't sleep well last night?"

"You could say that."

"Why?"

She looked at her hands in her lap. "I had a nightmare."

"Understandable," he said, keeping his voice steady. Fighting the urge to hold her.

"I'm scared, Jack. More now than I was before. If it's the Mafia, that's big. Really big." She met his gaze again, her blue eyes so troubled it hurt him. "What if I can't go home again? I mean ever?"

"This won't go on forever," he said. "I won't let it."

"What can *you* do?"

He took a sharp breath as the words stabbed him right in the chest. "The bullet wasn't to the brain," he said.

She shook her head. "That's not what I meant. I know you're good at your job. I meant, what can one man do? You have to admit you're pretty outnumbered."

"There's Frank and Bob."

"Big whoop. That makes three."

His wounded ego settled down as he realized what she was saying. She was right. Three cops weren't a hell of a lot. Three hundred cops would be better. But until he knew who was involved, he couldn't get more help. He'd thought about going to the captain, but even that was dangerous. "We'll figure it out, Hailey."

She nodded, but without conviction.

He reached over and took her hand, and he was immediately taken aback by how small and delicate she felt. How could these hands have given him that powerful massage? But he'd have to think about that later. "Listen," he said. "No matter what, I'll make sure you and Megan are safe. I won't let anything happen to you."

She looked at him for a long time, her gaze so steady he felt she was seeing more than just his face. It was as if she could see inside him. Making sure he was telling her the truth. "I believe you," she said finally.

"Good." He tried to withdraw his hand, but she held it more tightly, not letting him go.

"Jack?"

"Yes?"

"Would you do me a favor?"

"Sure."

"Can we just sit here for a little while? Not for long."

"I'm not going anywhere."

She smiled, and her cheeks turned a light pink. "Would you mind if I got a little closer to you?

He wanted to say yes. He minded very much. But he couldn't. She'd been through so much. All she was asking for was a little comfort. It was the least he could give her.

He gently pulled his hand away, then put it on the back of her neck. "Come on."

She scooted toward him, just like Megan had this afternoon. And he was just as uncomfortable as he'd been this afternoon, but for a very different reason.

As she snuggled against him and he felt the softness of her body, the struggle began in earnest. The wanting grew stronger as she nuzzled her head against his shoulder until she found the right spot.

He lowered his arm and held her close, tried not to think. Not to wish. Not to need.

He failed.

Chapter Twelve

Hailey woke up thinking about Jack. How he'd held her in his arms with so much tenderness it made her want to weep. And how she finally did weep, thinking about Megan, about the terrible men who wanted to hurt her. And how she'd looked into Jack's eyes, wanting to be closer still. Wanting to make love with him.

She turned over to check on Megan, but the girl wasn't in their bed. Hailey threw back the covers and got up, wondering if Jack was already awake, too. She needed to shower, but first, she needed to make sure Megan was all right.

She grabbed her stepfather's robe from the closet. It was so large she almost wrapped it twice around her. When she left the bedroom, she saw that Jack's door was still closed, and she heard Megan's voice in the living room.

Tiptoeing, she went down the hall until she could see Megan on the floor, playing on her quilt. The story hadn't changed, and Hailey supposed it never would. *The little girl finds herself alone, and she goes to the store where she reads her book and looks at pictures and...*

Hailey's heart thumped against her ribs. She moved closer, looking carefully at the quilt. Some pictures had blue borders, some had red and some had none at all. But when Megan told her story, it was always about the pictures in the red borders. Nothing else.

Something was there, right on the edge of Hailey's awareness. She studied each panel, went over the story word for word.

And then she got it.

She whirled around and headed back down the hall, adrenaline surging through her body. She got to Jack's door and knocked loudly. Urging him to be up, to let her in.

"Yeah?" he said, his voice groggy with sleep.

"Can I come in?"

"Yeah," he repeated. Hailey knew he wouldn't be groggy for long. Not after she told him.

He'd sat up, bolstering his back and head with his pillows. The covers had fallen to his waist. He wasn't wearing pajamas. But she couldn't think about that now.

"What's up?" he asked, rubbing his eyes with his knuckles.

"I've figured it out," she said, almost hopping in her excitement.

"Figured what out?"

"Where it is. The thing they're looking for."

"Huh? What are you talking about?"

She crossed to his bed and sat down facing him.

"You know the story Megan's always telling. The one where she uses the pictures on her quilt?"

He nodded, and she could see that the sleep had left him. He was sharp again.

"It's not just a story. It's a rebus."

"A re-what?"

"A rebus. A story told in pictures. But it's not just any story. The store? It's not just a store. It's a storage locker."

"I'm not following you."

"Get up," she said. "Get dressed. I'll show you."

She stood, her mind going a hundred miles an hour, thinking about each panel, each red-bordered picture. It was true. It had to be. But there were still some things missing. The name of the storage place. The key. But they'd figure it out. They would. Oh, why didn't he get up?

"Hailey."

"What?" she said, her voice high and animated.

"Unless you want a show of your very own, get out of here."

"Oh, yeah," she said, remembering he was naked. Wondering… No. Talk about the wrong time and the wrong place. And yet…

"Well?"

"I'm going, I'm going. But hurry."

"I will as soon as you—"

"Get out. Okay. Sheesh."

She left the bedroom and hurried to her own room. She washed up in record time, not even bothering with her hair, and pulled on a pair of jeans and a sweater. Shoes would wait.

She almost crashed into Jack as she went into the hall again. He steadied himself using the wall, and then he was fine again. Smiling her apology, she led him to the living room. Megan was still on the quilt.

"Honey?" Hailey said. "Would you do me a favor?"

Megan looked up. She was still in her pajamas. They were adorable, printed with little dancing teddy bears.

"Can you stand up and tell the story to Jack?"

Megan looked to Jack, then back at Hailey. Then, holding Tottie by the leg, she got to her feet. She started the familiar tale, beginning with a little girl all alone.

Hailey felt Jack at her shoulder, and as Megan went through each step of the story, Hailey found herself looking more at Jack than at the quilt. He listened carefully, his focus completely on the girl and the pictures. She saw the moment the lightbulb went on, the second he'd realized the importance of the quilt. Megan's parents had told her the story as a precaution. As a legacy. It spelled out, in pictures and letters, that something important was in storage, waiting for her.

"Look," Jack said to Hailey, leaning toward her. "The bees. Why are there bees at the store? You have a phone book?"

She hurried over to the table by the couch and opened up the drawer, pulling out the Yellow Pages. She flipped to the entries on storage facilities and ran her finger down the alphabet. She didn't have to go far. "Here," she said. "Bee's Storage. On Hill-croft."

Jack nodded. "Okay. So now, what about the key?"

She tore out the page and then went back to Jack's side. She looked at the hand-stitched picture of an old-fashioned skeleton key. It was right next to a heart, made of soft pink cotton. The heart had a key-hole.

Hailey stared, remembering how she'd played Concentration when she was a little girl. It was a board game her mother had given her, based on an old television show. A familiar phrase was covered by blank game pieces, and as each piece was re-moved, a part of the puzzle showed. The object was to solve the puzzle with as few uncovered clues as possible. Hailey had always been good at it, but she had to admit, this clue eluded her.

"Could the key be in the quilt?" Jack asked.

Hailey bent down and felt the square. Nothing but batting inside. She turned to Megan. "Sweetie?"

"Uh-huh?" Megan said softly.

"Did your mommy or daddy ever tell you about the key?" Hailey pointed to the picture.

Megan nodded.

Hailey felt her pulse shoot up again. "What did they tell you, honey?"

"That the key would open the magic box."

Hailey's hope deflated as she realized Megan didn't know any more than the story she'd learned by rote. "That's wonderful, Megan. Thank you."

"Hailey?" Megan asked.

"Yes?"

"Is it breakfasttime yet?"

Hailey smiled. "You bet it is. You want anything special?"

Megan nodded. "Cheerios."

"You got it." She stood up, then looked at Jack, who was still studying the rebus. "I'll put on some coffee and feed us. Then we'll think about this some more."

"Okay," he said, but she doubted he'd even heard her. His gaze didn't even flicker. "Where else have we seen a heart?" he asked.

She thought about that as she went to get Megan's breakfast. "I don't remember seeing anything in the pillowcase."

"We weren't looking for a heart, though. I think we should look again."

"You know where it is?"

He nodded, then headed off toward her bedroom. Hailey couldn't help but notice his limp was even worse than it had been yesterday. Which made sense. It was bound to be worse before it got better. But that wasn't going to stop her from pushing him to do his exercises today. And every day after that, until he could walk without that blasted cane.

She felt as though she'd uncovered a secret about Jack, too. It was only a piece of the puzzle, but it was a big piece. He hadn't taken her to his bed, even when she'd practically thrown herself at him. Not because he didn't want her. She was pretty sure of that. The look in his eyes had been enough to convince her. He didn't take the next step because he was embarrassed about his physical impairment. He felt less of a man because of it.

Last night she'd wanted to talk to him about it, but she'd chickened out. She wondered if she'd ever feel comfortable enough with him to broach the subject. She had the feeling it would be a difficult talk. One that would test both of them.

She got the Cheerios from the cupboard and put the box on the table just as Megan was climbing onto her chair. "Did you wake up a long time ago, Megan?"

The little girl looked up at her and nodded.

"Did something scare you?"

She nodded again.

"Want to talk about it?"

Megan didn't nod this time. She just gazed up at Hailey with eyes that held more hurt and fear than any four-year-old should have to feel.

Hailey pulled her chair next to Megan's and sat. "Was it a dream, honey?"

Megan's bottom lip started to quiver and her eyes welled with tears. "Someone hurt my daddy."

"That must have been very scary," Hailey said, taking her little hand.

"He died."

"Oh, sweet pea. I know. It's really awful. And it hurts. But don't worry. It won't always hurt this much."

"Will he come back?"

Hailey shook her head slowly. "No. He won't. But that doesn't mean he's stopped loving you. He's watching you right now from up in heaven. And he doesn't want you to be sad.''

''Is my mommy watching me, too?''

''Yes, she is. She loves you very much.''

Megan sniffed. ''I wish they were here.''

''They wish they were here, too.''

''Okay,'' Megan said, wiping her eyes with the sleeve of her pajamas.

''Better?'' Hailey asked.

Megan nodded. Then she looked at Hailey again. ''Can we really get a kitty?''

Hailey smiled. ''I promise.''

''Can I help pick her out?''

''You betcha.''

Megan smiled a little. Hailey kissed her on the nose, then went to get her a bowl, a spoon and the milk. After Megan was settled, Hailey made a pot of coffee, wondering if Jack was having any luck.

Discovering what was inside Bee's storage locker held the promise of solving all their problems. Whatever it was, she would give it to them. To the police or the Mafia or whoever it was who wanted to hurt Megan. She'd give it to them without a second thought if it would keep Megan safe. And if they had to disappear after that, so be it. Just like Barry Strangis had changed his name, so could she. There simply wasn't too high a price to pay to save Megan. Even if it meant leaving all she knew behind.

And Jack. She would go even if it meant she'd never see him again.

As if her thoughts had conjured him up, Jack walked into the kitchen carrying the pillowcase. He didn't look as if he'd figured out the mystery of the key. But maybe he'd think better after he had breakfast.

She got out the frying pan, the eggs and the bread, and got busy fixing a couple of omelets.

"I didn't see anything," Jack said. "Nothing. The recipe doesn't say anything about a key or a heart. I went through all her clothes. I don't get it."

Hailey watched as he took every item out of the pillowcase and put them on the table. The clothes, the picture, the recipe. Her gaze went to the photograph of Megan's mother. Maybe they shouldn't have it out now. Not after her conversation with Megan.

She lowered the flame beneath the pan, then went to pick up the photograph. Before she touched it, Jack's hand snapped over her wrist.

"Hold it."

"What?"

"A heart," he said. Then he let her go and picked up the picture frame. He put it upside down on the table, and carefully moved all the brads that held the back. He lifted that off, then the piece of cardboard.

She saw it at the same time Jack did. A key. Taped to the back of Patricia's picture. Right under her heart.

THEY REACHED the storage facility at just after two that afternoon. As Jack flashed his badge, the man in the front office ogled Hailey, making her incredibly uncomfortable. He also kept sniffing and it was a weird, almost nasty sound. She held Megan close to her, counting the seconds until they could get out of there.

Jack had the guy get the records for the locker registered to Roy Chandler. It took him a long time. Long enough for Megan to get fidgety and for Hailey to get scared. What if the bad guys had found out about the locker? What if they had someone watching this place, waiting for her to show up? They shouldn't have brought Megan. That was stupid. But what else could they have done?

The thing was, Jack couldn't do this by himself. She had to act as his legs, even though he hated to admit it. There was no way he could carry anything big out of the locker. Hailey kept feeling as if someone was pointing a gun at the small of her back. Or worse, at Megan.

The man, who hadn't given them a name, came back with a small plain folder. She looked over Jack's shoulder as he went through the material.

Roy had rented the locker three years ago. He'd paid cash. He'd also paid for the next three years, in cash, in advance. The receipt was dated two weeks ago.

Jack asked for photocopies of all the paperwork. The man behind the counter took his sweet time about it.

Megan tugged at Hailey's hand. "I want to go."

"I know, honey. It'll just be a few more minutes."

"It smells bad in here."

Hailey hoped the man hadn't heard that. But Megan was right. It did smell bad. She didn't even want to guess why.

Finally Jack got his copies, as well as directions to the storage locker. Hailey took in a big breath of fresh air as soon as they got outside.

The whole way back to the car, she felt herself growing more and more uneasy. As soon as they were all inside the car, Hailey locked all the doors. Of course, the glass wouldn't stop bullets, would it.

"You okay?" Jack asked.

"No, not really."

"It won't be long now," he said as he drove toward the back of the lot.

"It's just that..." She looked behind her at Megan and decided not to voice her fears.

"I know," Jack said. He found her hand and squeezed it, and Hailey felt instantly better. Not great, but better. She could never have done this without him. Not in a million years.

He parked the car directly in front of the narrow brick locker. No other cars were around, and when they got out and shut the Cadillac doors, the sound echoed, bouncing off the metal doors.

Jack got out the key and she found herself holding her breath as he slipped it into the lock. The click was audible. The key worked.

He opened the door and they went inside.

It was dark, but Hailey saw a string hanging from a bulb in the ceiling. She pulled it and the room lit up. At first she thought they'd screwed up or some-one had gotten there before them. But then she saw it. A bag, in the corner, sitting atop a bench. It was a large duffel bag, dark green. Nothing special about it.

Megan hesitated as Hailey started toward it. "What's wrong, Megan?" Hailey asked, crouching down to face her.

"I don't like it here."

"Neither do I," Hailey said. "So we're going to be as quick as possible, okay?"

Megan nodded cautiously.

Hailey picked her up. She was heavy, but nothing Hailey couldn't handle.

Jack was already at the bag. She could hear the sound of the zipper, loud in the empty space. Then she heard his soft whistle.

She hurried over to him and looked down. No wonder he'd whistled. The bag was filled with money. Neat stacks of hundred-dollar bills. She couldn't even guess how much was there, but it was a lot. "Holy cow," she said.

Jack pulled out a stack and fanned through it. "It's all hundreds," he said.

"How much do you think that is?" she asked.

"A couple hundred thousand maybe."

"So what was he keeping it here for?"

Jack didn't answer. He took out stack after stack of bills, piling them up on the bench. Every time she figured he'd reached the bottom, he found another layer. It reminded her of Mary Poppins's carpetbag.

"Okay," Jack said, almost to himself. At the bottom of the bag was a book. A black ledger. About the size of a hardback novel.

He pulled it out of the bag and opened it.

"What is it?"

He shook his head. "I don't know. It's some kind of code."

"Well, let's pack up and get out of here," she said. "We can look at it when we get home."

He nodded. He put the book to the side, then re-stuffed the duffel bag. When all the money was in, he put the book on top and zipped the bag closed.

Jack lifted the bag, but it was heavy and it wasn't easy for him. She didn't offer to help, though. She just followed him to the door.

He looked outside and then waved them out to the car. While Hailey buckled Megan into her car seat, he put the bag in the trunk. Five minutes later they were back on Hillcroft, heading toward the freeway.

"Well," Hailey said, "at least we know why they were after him."

Jack shook his head. "I don't think it's about the money. I think it's about the book."

"That was an awful lot of money," she said. "And who knows how much there was originally?"

"Which makes it curious that he lived in our apartment building," Jack said. "I mean if you had that kind of dough, would you?"

She shook her head. "Not unless I was trying to lie low. To be as invisible as possible."

"Okay, I'll give that to you. I'm still convinced there's more to it than cash."

"I don't disagree," she said. "But why do you think so?"

He looked at her for a long moment, then back at the road. "Call it a hunch. I just can't see the police getting involved in this for that kind of money. Even if it was a million bucks, they wouldn't risk it.''

"But they would for the book?"

He nodded. "That's my bet."

She shook her head. "Do you think it's evidence? I mean of the police and the Mafia working together?"

He raised a brow. "That would explain a lot, wouldn't it?"

"It would also make that book a very dangerous thing to have."

He nodded slowly, and Hailey felt a chill go down her spine. What had Barry Strangis gotten them all involved in?

Chapter Thirteen

Jack got the book out of the duffel bag and sat down on the couch. He didn't open it yet, even though he was curious as hell about it. He waited for Hailey to get back from her room. Megan had been so tired and cranky by the time they'd reached home that Hailey had put her down for a nap. It hadn't been pretty. Megan threw a world-class tantrum, right down to the kicking and screaming. All he'd wanted to do was get away, but Hailey stuck to her guns, patiently letting Megan know that there was no room for negotiation and that screaming wasn't going to work. It took a while, but finally the girl stopped fighting it, probably because she'd worn herself out. By the time Hailey carried her to the bedroom, she could barely keep her eyes open.

The second they were out of the room, his thoughts went to the murder. It hadn't been a shake-down. It had been an execution. The killer hadn't asked any questions. And yet, they'd torn up his apartment and come after Megan. Why? Why hadn't they beaten the information out of Chandler? Or popped him in the kneecap or something equally gruesome but effective?

It didn't make sense.

He studied the book cover. It wasn't anything special. No writing, just plain paper between some plastic-covered cardboard.

He looked at the hallway again, his impatience getting the better of him. It wouldn't matter if he opened the damn thing. He'd already gotten a look back at the storage place.

But he couldn't. Which was ridiculous. He couldn't look because he knew she'd be upset if he looked without her. He also knew she wouldn't say anything about it. She wasn't a complainer. He tried to imagine Crystal coping with this situation, and he couldn't. Because Megan would have been with social services so fast it would have made his head spin. Because Crystal would have disassociated herself from anything to do with the murder. Crystal had one priority: Crystal.

Who was he kidding? He was the same way. As selfish as the day was long. So consumed with his own problems, the rest of the world hardly existed.

Hailey wasn't like that. She'd made him promise to do his exercises again today. And she'd make him keep that promise. Because unlike him, she gave a damn about another person. She had a good heart. That would probably get her into big trouble one day. If he didn't watch himself, that day would get here real fast.

At last he heard Hailey's footsteps in the hall.

"She's asleep," Hailey said, going to the couch and plopping down next to him. "Finally."

"You were good with her," he said.

She shrugged, then nodded at the book. "So? What's the scoop?"

"I don't know. I haven't looked yet."

"Why?"

"I waited for you."

The look she gave him made the waiting worth it. More than worth it. No woman had ever looked at him that way before. It did something to him. Something dangerous.

He coughed, then shifted his attention to the book. He opened it to the first page, holding it so they both could see.

A long string of what he assumed were initials ran down the page, each followed by a number. A large number. Some entries had checkmarks, some were underlined, and two were crossed out. Jack turned the page and found the same thing. He noticed that a couple of the entries had phone numbers with the Chicago area code. And most had a string of numbers and letters that he couldn't identify.

"There's a repeat," she said, pointing to the initials *PB*. "I saw it on the first page."

He flipped back. On the first page *PB* was followed by *72,000* and *4BB330*. On the second page, it was followed by *125,000* and the *4BB330* again. If the first number represented dollars, the amounts were major. He quickly flipped through the whole book, and sure enough, it was more than three-quarters full. If those numbers were amounts of money, which he was hard-pressed to dispute, conservatively, he'd have to say they were talking about millions. Many many millions.

"What's that?"

"Hmm?"

Hailey reached over and took the book, then turned to a page near the end. A newspaper clipping was stuck on a blank page. It was a picture, no caption. She lifted it up, but it wasn't glued. "Well, goodness," she said. "It's our friend Craig Faraday."

"Why aren't I surprised?" He reached for the paper, but she peered at it more closely, her brows knitting with concern.

"Jack, look at this." She pointed to a police officer standing behind Faraday.

"Yeah?"

"Doesn't he look familiar to you?"

Jack stared, trying to figure out what she meant. The guy was big, maybe in his late fifties. But his face didn't ring any bells.

"The cop," she said. "Back at Roy's apartment." She shook her head. "But he was younger. A lot younger."

Jack looked at the clipping again, trying to make some kind of ID on the guy, but the picture wasn't clear enough. Except... "You know, he does kinda look like Brett Nichols."

"What do you know about him?"

"He's a detective in vice. I didn't know him well. He hadn't been working very long before I had to leave. He moved here from somewhere."

Hailey looked at him, her eyes alight with discovery. "From Chicago?"

"I don't know. But I can find out."

Hailey fetched the phone, and she took the book and the press clipping while he dialed. He asked for Bob Dorran, hoping he was there and not out on some case.

"Dorran."

"Hey. It's Jack."

"How you doin' buddy?" Bob asked, lowering his voice.

"Fine. I want you to do something for me."

"Name it."

"You know that new guy, Brett Nichols?"

"In vice?"

"Yeah. Find out where he's from, would you? And find out if he's got any connection to Faraday."

There was a stretch of silence, and then Jack heard a woman's voice in the background. Probably Kelly, the chief's assistant.

"Listen, pal," Bob said, and from the way he sounded, Jack thought he was probably cupping his hand over the mouthpiece. "I don't know if this is such a good idea."

"Why not?" Jack asked, fighting the urge to whisper.

"Faraday isn't someone to mess with."

"Neither am I."

"He's got a lot of juice behind him, Jack. Why don't you just forget this thing, huh?"

"I can't." He laughed, but not because anything

was funny. "You try staying home and watching TV every day for three months."

"If you're bored, take up knitting. This isn't a hobby for a smart man. And if I remember correctly, your momma didn't raise any fools."

"No, she didn't. But she did raise a determined SOB."

Bob sighed. "All right. I'll find out what I can." He chuckled. "Between me and Frank, you have half the force doing your legwork."

"Yeah, well, I figure if the captain finds out, he'll thank me for keeping you guys out of the doughnut shop."

"Hey, Jack?"

Jack smiled as Bob told him where he and his doughnuts could go. Then he hung up and dialed Houston information. The operator gave him Faraday's number. It wasn't his home, though. She didn't have that. But if he needed it, Bob or Frank would find it for him.

"You're calling Faraday?" Hailey asked. "Isn't that dangerous?"

"Not if I do it right," he said as he punched in the number. A woman answered. A receptionist or secretary. Jack asked for Faraday. When she wanted to know who was calling, he said "Detective Regan. Houston PD."

Hailey's brows shot up at the lie, but he just smiled at her. Then he listened to an instrumental version of an Elton John song for a while. A long while.

"Faraday."

He sounded busy. Like a real tycoon. "Mr. Faraday, I'm Detective Regan for the Houston PD. I'd like to ask you a couple of questions."

"What's this regarding?"

"An ex-employee of yours. A Mr. Barry Strangis."

Faraday didn't say anything. He just breathed into the phone. "I vaguely remember someone by that name. But it was years ago."

"Yes, sir, it would be. I was wondering if you could give me any information about him. What he did for you. If you had anything to do with him going to jail. If he has any family."

"I don't know," Faraday said, sounding irritated. "I hardly remember the man."

There was a long pause, and Jack figured that was the end of it. But then he heard Faraday sigh.

"He was hired as a butler. He and his wife worked for me. She was the cook."

"And why did they leave your employ?"

"Because they stole close to twenty thousand dollars from me, that's why."

"I see."

"Don't you have that in your files?"

"Yes, but the data is sketchy. What about family?"

Jack waited. He could hold out as long as he needed to.

"He had a brother, I think. It's a long time ago, and I never paid that much attention to him when he worked for me. But I seem to recall a brother in Oklahoma. Tulsa."

"Is there anything else you can tell me about Mr. Strangis?"

"No. I don't know much about him. I haven't seen him in years. Oh—I also heard he had a daughter."

"Oh?"

"Yes. But then, I'm sure you know that already."

Jack coughed, but he didn't take the bait.

Finally he wore Faraday down. "Is that all, Detective?" he said, not bothering to hide his annoyance.

"One more thing. I hear you're moving your corporate offices?"

"Yes. Which is why I don't have a lot of time to chat."

"Are you moving out of the state?"

"No. We're moving downtown. Look, Regan, I need to go now. If you have any more questions, send me a letter and I'll have my secretary dig around, but I'm sure there's nothing else to be found."

"Thank you."

Faraday hung up without saying goodbye. Jack put the phone on the floor, then turned to Hailey. "There might be a brother."

Hailey cocked her head. "Do you think he was involved?"

"I don't know," he said. "But if he's there and he's a relative…"

She turned away, and he could see he'd really upset her. Her body language was tighter than it should be.

"Hailey? We need to find out the truth.

"I don't want to know," she said, whirling to face him.

He got his cane and struggled to his feet. "Yeah, you do. Because it's the right thing. Listen, I think you're good for her. And she's good for you. But you have to know the score. Be prepared. You're not going to be in hiding forever."

"You don't think so?"

He touched her arm and she didn't jerk away, which was a good sign. "No, I don't. This book, if it's what we think it is, is going to make a lot of people unhappy. But it's also gonna make a judge real interested in certain bank accounts."

"But that's just it. We don't know for sure."

"We'll find out. And when we do, we'll end this thing. And I'll make sure you and Megan are safe. You have my word on that."

"I want to believe you," she said softly.

"Have I ever lied to you before?"

That got a little smile out of her. "I have no idea."

"Trust me. I'm just like a friggin' Boy Scout."

She brought her hand to his face and gently caressed his cheek. Her gaze, only moments ago like steel, was now soft and caring. Too caring. But her hand felt damn good. Damn soft.

"What am I going to do with you?" she whispered.

He took her hand in his, stopping her. "You're going to be cautious, that's what. You have important business to take care of now. A little girl who's depending on you."

"That's not what I meant."

He looked away as he let go of her hand. "I know. But that's all I can offer you right now."

"Why?" she asked, moving until he was forced to meet her gaze again. "Why can't we have more?"

His gut tightened as he fought for control. As he struggled not to take her in his arms. He wanted to give her everything, but the truth was his "everything" wasn't a whole hell of a lot.

"Is it about that?" she asked, nodding at his cane.

"That's part of it."

"What else?"

"Hailey, we don't have time for this. I need to go to the station. I need to talk to Frank."

"Oh, no. You're not leaving now. I won't let you."

"What do you want from me?" he asked.

She stared at him for a few seconds, her gaze never wavering. "I don't know for sure. But I think...I think we might have something. Together."

"It's the circumstances. The forced togetherness. You're just afraid and—"

"Don't tell me what I feel or don't feel. Everyone always wants to tell me that. I understand about the circumstances. And I understand about your hip and about your job and everything else. And I'm still telling you I think there's something going on here. Something we need to explore."

He could feel his heart beat in his chest. The air fill his lungs. But all he wanted to feel was Hailey in his arms. In his bed. "I can't," he said, forcing the words out. Breaking the last of his spirit. "I can't."

"Bull. You won't. There's a big difference." She walked to the kitchen and got herself a glass, then banged the cupboard shut. She was mad, and he couldn't blame her. It had taken courage to say what she had. Courage he couldn't match.

He was a coward and he knew it. A sorry broken coward.

"Are you leaving?" she asked. She poured herself some bottled water and drank it down quickly.

"Yes."

"How long will you be gone?"

"I don't know. A few hours."

"And what if something happens? Then what?"

"I'll be fine."

"I wasn't talking about you. I was talking about Megan and me. What do we do if you don't come back?"

He moved to the kitchen counter and pulled over a small notepad. He wrote Frank's number, Bob's number and, just in case, Crystal's number. "You won't need these," he said.

She nodded, but she didn't look at the numbers. "All my life people have told me I wasn't good enough or smart enough or pretty enough. I've had to struggle for everything I've ever had. I won't beg you, Jack. If you say no, that's it."

He closed his eyes for a second, then looked at her, hardly believing that anyone could have said she wasn't smart or pretty. She was all that and so much more. But she wasn't for him. He was nothing but a burned-out shot-up selfish cop who wouldn't know how to have a good relationship if he tried. "For what it's worth," he said, "I think you're an incredible woman. In every way. And you deserve to have it all."

"All meaning, not you."

He nodded.

She sighed. "Go to the station," she said. "I want this thing solved. I want it over. And I want you gone."

He turned, cursing his luck. Cursing the bullet that had shattered his life.

He went to the door and put on his holster, then his jacket. He fished the keys from his pocket, and even though he was ready, he didn't open the door.

"Well?" she asked. "What are you waiting for?"

"I don't know," he said. "I hate leaving like this."

"Like what?"

"With you mad at me."

"I'm not mad," she said, as she walked toward him. "I'm disappointed. I'll get over it."

He remembered their kiss. The way she'd felt and her scent and the overwhelming urge he'd had to take her right there in the kitchen. The way he wanted her made him crazy. And that she thought she wanted him was just plain cruel.

But what he could see that she couldn't was what would happen after this case was over. After they left this house by the beach.

He had nothing. She deserved everything. It was as simple as that. "I'm sorry," he said.

"Me, too."

"I'll be back soon."

"Yeah." Then she turned and headed for the hallway. He walked out the door and locked it behind him. A bolt of lightning lit up the sky and thunder followed, a crash from the gods, a smash of Thor's hammer. A fitting score for the wreckage that was his life.

Chapter Fourteen

Hailey looked in on Megan to find her sleeping soundly. She had her arm around Tottie's neck in a comforting embrace. Just looking at her made Hailey feel like crying.

But the tears she held back weren't for Megan. They were for her. And for Jack. He was so frustrating! The attraction was mutual, that much she was sure about. She'd never been more positive of anything. There was something remarkable going on between them, and she knew if they played it out, it would change both their lives.

She'd never been bolder with a man. She'd certainly never set herself up for rejection like this before. But something told her he was worth the fight.

As she went back into the living room, her gaze fell on a picture of her mother. She certainly hadn't learned much about good relationships from her. She'd bickered constantly with all her husbands. It was a terrible thing to grow up with, and she wasn't spared their vicious tongues, either. All her life she'd had her failings pointed out. If she came home with a B on her report card, her mother asked why it wasn't an A. She'd wanted to try out for the softball team at her high school, but after her father had told her how inept she was and how she'd never be a real player, she'd given it up. They hadn't approved of her friends, which made for a very lonely childhood. By the time she was eighteen, she was afraid to try anything.

Looking back, it was easy to see why she'd settled for Steven. He was so much like her parents, always negative, always demeaning. It was painful, but it was a familiar pain.

Leaving him, starting her web-site-design business and keeping her distance from her parents had taken all her strength. The voices in her head were a constant. Whenever she tried anything new, she heard her mother's disdainful chuckle or her father's sharp ridicule. It was as much a part of her as her hair or her eyes.

Until now. Until Jack. When she was with him, the voices stilled. The incessant second-guessing disappeared, and in its place came a strength she'd never known. The way he listened to her, the way Jack trusted her. It made her feel as if she could conquer the world. Or at the very least, it made her feel as if she could be a good mother to Megan, which was actually better.

And it made her feel like a woman a man could love.

Not that she thought Jack loved her. She knew it was too soon for that, but the possibility existed that he could love her. If he wanted to.

If he could get past his pride. Past his anger at the world.

She went into the kitchen and pulled out the chicken she'd defrosted, along with vegetables and rice. It would be a simple meal, but she knew Jack would compliment her on it. That he'd make a little fuss.

That was it of course. The reason she'd fallen. Well, one of the reasons. Because he made a little fuss over a simple meal. That he waited to open the ledger. Because he'd done his exercises for her.

The feelings scared her. They made her too vulnerable. If she wasn't careful, she'd be terribly hurt when this was over.

She sighed. Who was she kidding? She'd gone and done the stupidest thing. She'd fallen in love with Jack, and there wasn't a thing she could do about it.

THE RAIN LET UP just as Jack pulled into the department multilevel parking lot. He drove to the top level, preferring to keep his Cadillac as far away from curious stares as possible. After he parked, he sat there for a few minutes, staring out the windshield. Not at anything in particular. Just an old brick wall. But his thoughts were sharply in focus, maybe sharper than they'd ever been before.

What was he going to do about Hailey? The whole way into town, he'd tried to figure it out, and he was no closer to an answer almost an hour later.

It all boiled down to the inescapable fact that he'd been shot. If it had just been his limp, he probably could have gotten over it. But the bullet had taken away his job, his future, his identity. How could he love anyone if he didn't really exist? And he didn't. This farce of him investigating Chandler's murder was just that—a farce. Frank and Bob were doing the real work. Even Hailey had done more than him.

The only thing he was good for these days was clicking the remote and drinking beer. Nice. Nice thing to offer a woman like Hailey. A woman so fine he couldn't begin to think why she wanted him at all.

There was still time to show her the error of her ways. That she was enamored of an illusion, a badge without a man. He'd have to convince her that it was a mistake to think he could make her happy. He'd have to convince himself that it wouldn't kill him to succeed.

He pushed open the car door and went through the humiliating ritual of getting his cane, placing it exactly, then hoisting himself up. If he was smart, he'd get back in the car and drive west, and keep on driving until he hit the Pacific Ocean. Leave Hailey and Megan and this whole business to people who were equipped to handle it.

Instead, he headed for the elevator, and when it came he got in. He pressed the button for the lobby, wondering if Frank or Bob would be there. Hoping they wouldn't. He'd hate seeing the look of pity in their eyes.

JACK TURNED ON his computer and waited for the boot sequence to finish. He'd dodged several cops he didn't want to see and made it to his desk, or what used to be his desk, with only one or two people knowing he was here.

He wanted to look up the initials in the book. To see if he could make sense of them. *GW,* for example, might be George Winslow, the police commissioner. On the other hand, *GW* might be some unlucky schmuck who'd bet too heavily on a Rockets game.

His plan was to look up city government and police officials, and print up some lists he could take back home. Then he'd see if the numbers meant anything—the nine numbers he thought might be social-security numbers. That would do it. That would be enough to get a search warrant and start a full investigation. He'd already decided he'd go to the FBI. No sense risking everything talking to the wrong cop.

He typed his name and his password, anxious to get in and get out. But a notice appeared, instead of a menu. A notice that said his password was no good.

So that was the way it was going to be. They'd told him he could have a desk job until he got back on his feet, but they'd lied. They knew he'd never be back. That he was a washed-up cripple of no use to anyone.

He turned off the computer and reached for his cane.

"Hold on there, Jackson."

He looked up at the sound of Frank's voice. Despite Jack's earlier wish, he was glad to see a friendly face. To know that at least someone hadn't forgotten about him. "How you doin', Sparky?" Jack asked, using his nickname from the police academy.

"I gotta go to the can," he said. "Why don't you hobble with me?"

"You're just as suave as ever," Jack said, ignoring his own feelings of embarrassment as he leaned on his cane.

"Why tamper with perfection?"

Jack shook his head as he followed Frank past a row of cubicles, down a hall and into the men's room. As soon as they were inside, Frank held up a cautionary hand.

He went to each stall and checked to make sure no one was there. Then he went back to the door and flipped the lock.

"First, Brett Nichols. Something's up with him. He's been on the force for two years, and he's not moving up the ranks very fast. He got in because of his father. A twenty-eight year veteran who now works for guess who?"

"Faraday."

"Score one for the gimp."

Jack nodded, thinking about Faraday, about Nichols, and about what the hell Megan could have that they'd want.

"Second, what the hell are you doing here?" he asked, turning to face Jack. His bonhomie had gone, leaving him the tough cop Jack knew him to be.

"I came to use the computer," he said, "but my password didn't work. They've locked me out."

"I'm not surprised," Frank said, pulling out a pack of cigarettes. He wasn't actually going to smoke, because that was against the law, but as long as Jack had known him, he liked to hold a cigarette between his fingers. Sometimes he'd have one anchored behind his ear, one in his hand and one dangling from the corner of his mouth. Jack had learned a long time ago to keep his mouth shut. Everyone deserves a crutch.

"There's been talk about you. You really shouldn't have come."

"Talk? What kind?"

Frank shrugged. "I don't know. They don't include me. Everyone knows we're friends. But everyone's wondering why you're not at home. Why you disappeared the day after the murder at your apartment."

"Screw 'em," Jack said, angrier about his computer privileges being taken away than being a suspect in the murder.

"That's easy for you to say," Frank said. "But you'd better be careful. This thing could get messy."

"What do you know?"

Frank shook his head. "Bob is checking on Faraday. I've been stuck on another case, but we were going to get together tonight and figure out what's what."

"Okay," Jack said. "I'll copy down the information I need you to get, and I'll bring it back tomorrow."

"Don't. You've got a computer with a modem, don't you? I mean, where you're staying?"

Jack nodded.

"I'll give you my password," Frank said. "Log in as me tonight. I won't be using the computer. No one will know the difference."

"I'm not sure I can get the stuff I need over the modem."

"Try. And if you don't have any luck, we'll go to plan B."

"What might that be?" Jack asked.

"Hell, I don't know. Pull back and punt."

Jack smiled. Then someone came to the washroom door and tried to open it. After two good tugs the gentleman outside started banging on the door. Loudly.

"We'd better get out of here," Frank said. "I'll walk you to your car."

"You don't have to."

"I know it, dummy. I want to." Frank opened the door, and a rather desperate-looking uniformed officer rushed past them to the far stall.

"When you gotta go…" Jack started.

"You gotta go." Frank finished.

HAILEY TURNED ON her laptop. Megan had been asleep for almost two hours, and Hailey debated waking her so she would sleep through the night. She decided to wait a little while longer. She hadn't answered e-mail in ages, and she shuddered to think what was waiting for her. She wanted to see if any of her clients needed updates. This was no time to lose business, not with what lay ahead.

Once the connection was made, she went into her mail program and started at the beginning. Forty-seven e-mails sat waiting to be read.

The first three were updates on web pages she did for a group of mystery writers. The next e-mail was just a notice that her credit card had been billed for her monthly fee. She clicked on the next, but before she could read it, the oven timer went off. She got up from the kitchen table and put on some oven mitts, then took out the chicken casserole. It smelled heavenly. She turned off the oven and went back to her chair, thinking about making a salad to go with dinner.

Then her gaze went to her screen and all thoughts of dinner evaporated as an icy chill went down her back.

It was a message, and it was right to the point: *Give us the girl or we'll take her. You won't like how. Bring her to your apartment tonight at 10:30. We won't hurt her if you do as we say.* It wasn't signed of course. But it was dated two nights ago.

So they'd found her web site. She'd been thorough when she'd registered the site with all the search engines. It must have been remarkably easy for them. She broke out in gooseflesh and her heart thudded. Why wasn't Jack here? Why hadn't he left her a gun?

She got up and raced to Megan's room. The little girl hadn't budged. Hailey went to the window, even though she remembered locking it. She checked, trying to pull the window up, but the lock held. Then she went to Jack's room, then the bathroom and finally back to the windows in the living room and kitchen, checking every one. The door was bolted and the curtains were all drawn. Logic told her that they didn't know where she was. She'd know it if they had. That just because they'd located her e-mail address, it didn't mean they would find *this* address.

She was safe, at least for the moment. But she wished that Jack would hurry.

JACK LET FRANK out of the elevator first. Then he walked toward his car, his friend to the right of him. Dark clouds made it feel later than four-thirty. It would rain again soon, which would make his drive back to Galveston a nightmare. Especially at rush hour.

"So how's that hip of yours?" Frank asked.

Jack shook his head. "The same."

"You doin' what the doc told you to?"

Jack nodded. "Yes, sir. I'm doing everything I'm supposed to."

"Good. 'Cause I don't like it when you're not on my team, buddy. We need you back."

"Don't count on it. You know what I'm up against."

Frank waved his hand dismissively. "We'll get these slimeballs," he said. "Then you'll come back and everything will be the same."

Jack knew it wouldn't. Even if they did solve the case, things wouldn't be back to normal. Because he couldn't go back. He would never be able to put this behind him.

Frank took the cigarette he'd perched behind his ear and lit it, taking a deep inhalation of smoke and nicotine. He sighed, blowing the smoke out.

"You ever gonna quit that—" Jack froze. Something was wrong. He went for his gun, and then he heard the pop-pop of gunfire spitting from a silencer.

Frank dropped like a ton of bricks and Jack dived behind a Buick Skylark.

A bullet slammed into the windshield of the car, shattering it into a spiderweb of broken glass, still attached to the window. He couldn't see anything—except Frank's motionless body.

Not again, he thought.

He was on his side, his cane next to Frank. Jack pulled himself up on the car bumper as he listened for the sound of feet on the pavement. Nothing.

An image of Hailey flashed into his head and he felt his chest constrict. What would she do if he didn't get back to Galveston? How could he protect her if he was dead?

The sound of a car engine revving chased his thoughts away, leaving him focused and steady. The only problem was, his body wouldn't be able to do anything, even if there was something to do. He was trapped, like a fly in amber. The bastards could pick him off any way they chose.

The engine cranked up another notch, then tires squealed, and Jack saw a gray Pontiac shoot out from behind a pillar. He ducked as the car sped by, knowing he couldn't do more if they decided to shoot him. But they didn't. They went right into the curve of the down-ramp, leaving him sweating in the cold air.

He lurched over to Frank, expecting a lot of blood. But there wasn't any. At least not that he could see. He reached down to turn him over, but Frank sat up, shaking his head. ''What happened?''

''I thought you were dead.''

Frank touched his chest and his legs, searching for a wound. "If I wasn't hit, what happened to me?"

Jack nodded at his friend's head. "There," he said. "You're bleeding."

Frank touched his temple, then brought his hand down again to look at the dark red blood. "Bullet must have grazed me."

"Damn lucky," Jack said. "Another inch and you'd be meeting your maker."

Frank cursed, his voice still a little shaky. He got up, grabbing Jack's cane as he stood. "Here. You'd better get out of here before someone comes and starts asking questions."

"You sure you're okay?"

"I'm fine. Don't worry about me. Go on. It's late, and it's gonna take you a couple hours to get home from here. The ferry's gonna be murder. Bob and I will take care of things out here."

Jack stuck out his hand, and Frank grabbed it. They shook, but then Frank stepped forward and gave him a bear hug. Then he let go, and stared down at the pavement.

Jack walked to his car and got in. He started her up, but before he pulled out, he looked at Frank. The man just stood there, blood dripping down his face. Then the rain came, and it washed his face clean.

Jack put the car in gear and left the station. He knew it was the last time he'd see the station. Someone there had arranged to have him killed. It could be anyone from the cop that needed the washroom to the captain. If he was to go back, his life wouldn't be worth a plugged nickel. Which wasn't a big deal, except that he needed to be there for Hailey. Except that he *wanted* to be there for Hailey.

Of all the damn times to start caring.

Chapter Fifteen

Hailey almost jumped out of her skin when she heard the dead bolt click open. She grabbed a knife from the counter, prepared to kill or be killed. Then she saw it was Jack. Of course. Jack. She sighed, willing her heart to slow down.

He shut the door behind him, then looked at her curiously. "What's that for?"

"I wanted to protect myself," she said. She looked down to see that, instead of the knife she thought she'd grabbed, she was pointing a potato peeler at him.

"Were you planning to peel me to death?"

"If I had to."

He smiled. "I'd hate to run into you in a dark alley."

"Next time I won't be so nice," she said. "I'll get out the melon baller."

"Ouch."

"You betcha."

He hung up his jacket and took off his holster, then

he looked around the living room. "Where's Megan?"

"She's playing in the bedroom. I'm just finishing dinner, so go wash up. And wash Megan, too, please."

"Let's talk first," he said. "While she's out of the room."

"What happened?" she asked, instantly nervous. She'd planned on telling him about the e-mail message after dinner, but if he'd had a message, too…

"Someone took a shot at me."

Her adrenaline kicked up again, but she kept her cool. "Go sit down," she said. She got him a cold beer from the fridge and went to sit with him on the couch.

"I don't know, Hailey," he said resignedly. "I don't know that you're safe here anymore. Isn't there somewhere else you could go? Like Timbuktu?"

She shook her head. "This is it. The only place I know."

"It's not safe." He caught her gaze and held it. "They know I'm involved. They're going to assume I have Megan. And I wouldn't doubt that they know you're with me."

"They do," she said, curling her legs under her.

"What do you mean?"

"I mean they sent me a message."

He sat forward, squeezing the beer bottle so tightly his fingers turned white. "How?"

"By computer. They know my e-mail address. They must have done a search on me and found my web site. My e-mail address is right on it."

"What did the message say?"

"They want Megan. They told me to bring her back to my apartment, but that was two nights ago."

"What was the return address?"

She shook her head. "I tried to search it, but it had already been disconnected. It was one of those free things from Juno."

He cursed soundly, his frustration making the muscles in his jaw tighten. "Did you print it out?"

She went to the kitchen table, picked up a sheet of paper and handed it to him.

He looked at it for a long minute, then put it down. "Frank and I were walking to my car," he said. "There were three shots, maybe four. I thought Frank had been killed because he dropped like a stone. But his head had only been grazed."

"And you?"

He looked down as if he was ashamed to speak. "I'm fine. I'm perfectly fine."

"You didn't hurt your hip?"

He took a long swallow of beer, then wiped his mouth. He stared at her, but she had the feeling he wasn't seeing her. It was difficult not to press him, but she held her tongue. She just waited.

"I want to do the exercises," he said finally. "Tonight."

"We can wait till tomorrow. You've been through enough excitement today."

"No. I want to do them tonight. After dinner. And then we'll figure out what we're going to do."

She wasn't sure why this had been his response. But she could hazard a guess. He'd felt helpless and he couldn't stand it. She hated that it took something so dangerous to motivate him, but she wasn't going to argue with the result. "All right," she agreed. "Right after dinner."

He put his hand on her knee. "Are you okay?"

She nodded. "As long as I have my potato peeler, I'm not worried."

That made him smile. And lean toward her. Her eyes fluttered closed as she waited for his kiss, but it didn't come. He cleared his throat, took back his hand, shifted away.

She got up to put dinner on the table.

HE WATCHED HAILEY put pajamas on Megan, but he wasn't interested in the child. His focus was on the woman. He studied each feature carefully. Her hair, her eyes, her nose. When he got to her mouth, he stopped breathing. The thought of kissing her, of holding her, spurred more dangerous thoughts. Maybe she wouldn't mind the scars. Or that he was on disability. Maybe she could overlook his limp and his cane.

Who was he kidding? Hailey was a woman, not a saint. She might be able to ignore his problems at first, but it wouldn't last. She'd wake up one morning and see him for what he was, and she'd hate him for tricking her.

He couldn't do that to her. Not her. She laughed and the sound moved through him, stirring something warm deep inside.

If she had been anyone else, he'd make a move and damn the consequences. If she had been anyone else, he wouldn't care that he had to move gingerly or that she'd probably have to do most of the work.

But he couldn't stand it if she pitied him.

"Someone wants to say good-night," Hailey said as she and Megan came over to the couch.

"Oh, yeah? Who?" he asked, glancing at Megan and trying to look very serious.

"Me," she said.

"Me, who?"

"Me, Megan."

"Megan who?"

"Megan Chandler."

"Hmm," he said, rubbing his chin. "Megan Chandler. Have I ever met her?"

Megan giggled and looked up at Hailey. "He's funny."

"You're right," Hailey said. "He's very funny."

Megan let go of Hailey's hand and got up on the couch next to him. Then, leaving Tottie on the cushion beside him, she climbed onto his lap, facing him. She put her little hands on his cheeks. So tiny, so warm, so unexpected, he had to swallow a lump in his throat.

"You've met me," she said solemnly. "I'm the little girl who lives here."

"Oh," he said. "*That* Megan."

She giggled again, leaned forward and kissed him gently on the lips. Then she leaned back. "Your face is scratchy."

"Oh, I don't think so," he said. "I think your hands are scratchy."

"Uh-uh. Look." She held up her hands, palms front, proving her statement unequivocally.

"My mistake," he said.

She leaned sideways to get Tottie, then brought the doll up to his face. "Tottie wants a kiss goodnight, too."

He blinked at the ratty doll, then up at Hailey. She was no help. She was grinning like the Cheshire cat.

"Can't I just kiss you again?"

Megan shook her head. "Tottie."

"Tottie," he repeated, grateful beyond words no cameras were around. He quickly kissed the doll, then smiled broadly, unwilling to let Megan know how silly he felt.

She nodded at him, then climbed off his lap. Once she was on the floor again, she said, "Hailey, if you ask him, he'll kiss you good-night, too."

"Thank you," Hailey said. "I'll do that. Now, let's get you and Tottie into bed."

The two of them walked away hand in hand, Tottie dragging across the carpet. What would it be like if they were his? If this wasn't a temporary unnatural situation?

He looked away, wiping the image from his mind as he struggled up to get the exercise mat. His hip hurt like hell, but he didn't care. He would do the work, whatever it took, even though he knew he'd never be completely whole. But at least he'd look normal on the outside. He'd work as hard as he had to, for as long as he had to.

It took him a while to get down on the floor, but fortunately Hailey was still in the bedroom with Megan. He moved his cane out of the way and began the first stretch, remembering to count to five, to breathe at the exertion, just as Hailey had told him to.

But he missed her voice. Her encouragement. The feel of her hand on his back.

God, what was the matter with him? He was acting like a lovesick boy and for what? Wanting her was more painful than the bullet wound. He couldn't have her. He cared too much to do that to her.

HAILEY WATCHED HIM for a while, grateful that Megan had gone to sleep so quickly. She'd feared that her long nap would keep her up, but Megan surprised her. Hailey smiled, thinking about the little girl and how adorable she was. The truth was, she was in love with Megan. In love with her strength and her curly hair and the way she smelled. She wanted the girl for her own, and if something happened to take her away? She couldn't think of that. Not tonight.

Her gaze focused again on Jack. And the same swell of affection filled her, only the feelings she had for Jack were more complicated. Much more complicated. The way she felt about him was layered, some of it intellectual, but most of it quite primal. Just looking at him made her breasts ache to be touched, made her grow moist and needy.

But she couldn't do a damn thing about it. She'd already made a big enough fool of herself. No way she could stand to be rejected again. She wasn't strong enough.

Jack did his final stretch, which was her cue. She

knelt in front of him as he lay back. His chest rose and fell rapidly—he'd worked hard. She lifted his right leg, but instead of pushing it toward his chest, she pulled off his boot, then did the same with his left boot. He didn't say anything as she then brought his foot to her chest. He had on navy socks. She shifted his foot until it nestled between her breasts, and then she slowly pushed, forcing his leg up and back. She tried to count, but he was looking at her. His gaze went from her eyes to his foot and where she'd put it.

She leaned back, breaking the connection between them, at least the eye contact. But she couldn't shake off the arousal that had her chest rising and falling as if she'd just run a mile. She pushed again, unable to keep from meeting his gaze. Completely aware that he would see her desire. Prepared to have him do nothing about it. She was a fool and she knew it. And still she begged him with her eyes.

The game went on for a long time. She kept up her end of the bargain by helping him stretch his muscles. He worked with her, breathing when he was supposed to, relaxing even though she knew he was hurting.

All the while they said nothing with their mouths, but volumes with their eyes. With their bodies.

She told him of her need.

He answered with his hunger.

She blushed, but she didn't look away.

And he grew hard. Visibly hard.

Finally she finished and she started to move into the next position, but Jack sat up and grabbed her wrist. The game was over. He'd tell her to stop. To leave him be. She wouldn't cry. She *wouldn't*.

He pulled her toward him, his grasp so rough it hurt. But she didn't care. Then he kissed her, hard. Kissed her with all the desperation she'd felt, all the desire she'd been unable to fight.

She kissed him back, tasting him, breathing his scent, following him as he lay down until they were both on the mat and his arms were around her.

As his hand moved down her back, she shivered, loving his touch, wanting more. Much more. She broke the kiss and stilled his hand. "We can't do this here," she said. "Megan."

He nodded and propped himself up on his elbow. But then he paused and she saw his doubt. She could back off now, no harm done. She could make a joke, pretend it didn't matter. Instead, she stood and held out her hands. Urging him to take them. To let her help him.

For a long moment, long enough for her to wonder about her sanity, she stood there. And then his hands were in hers. She pulled him up, letting him lean lightly on her with his arm around her shoulder and hers around his waist. She smiled as she walked with him toward his bedroom.

Was it really her? Shy quiet Hailey? It couldn't be. But it was. He'd changed her. He'd made her bold.

They walked into his room and she kicked the door shut behind them. Then she helped him to the bed.

"Hailey," he said. "I don't know…"

"I do," she said. "So you just relax."

"I want it to be perfect. Perfect for you."

She smiled again. "It already is." She kissed him, ran her tongue over his lips, then pulled back. He started to unbutton his shirt, but she stopped him. "Relax," she whispered as she sank to her knees in front of him, spreading his legs apart so she could be closer.

She unbuttoned his shirt slowly, loving the feeling of power she had, the electricity that seemed to flow from her fingertips. She felt no embarrassment, no hesitation. Only pleasure, anticipation.

At the last button she pulled his shirt wide open and kissed his chest. As she worked to unbuckle his belt, she moved her lips to his nipple, flicking it with her tongue, making him moan.

Using only her sense of touch, she found the buttons on his jeans and undid them one by one. Then she sat back, admiring his strong chest, the line of dark hair that went down and down until it was hidden by his boxers. She smiled as she saw the evidence of his arousal, now unfettered by the heavy jeans. But she wanted to see everything. All of him.

She reached to touch him, but he stopped her. He took her wrists and raised her to her feet. Then he pulled her close, burying his head against her stomach, wrapping his arms tightly around her waist.

She rubbed her fingers through his dark hair, then down his back. Lifting his shirt, she caressed his bare flesh, amazed at his heat and his muscles.

He kissed her breast through the material of her sweater, then pulled back. He lifted the garment as high as he could, then she took over, pulling it up and off. She tossed it on the floor.

His hands moved behind her back until they met at the clasp of her bra. With a magician's deftness, he unhooked the clasp, then moved his hands to the straps, pulling them down until the bra came all the way off. She let it drop at his feet while he touched her. Gently, almost too gently, he rubbed his palms against her stiffened nipples until she was forced to lean into his hands. He cupped her, then brought his mouth to the dark aureole of her right breast.

She had to close her eyes as he teased her nipple with his tongue and his teeth, as he sucked and licked the tender flesh. Just when she couldn't stand it another minute, he moved to her left breast, where he paid the same exquisite homage.

Jack moved his hands to her leggings, snaking his fingers beneath the material, then pulling down. In one smooth motion, she was almost naked. She stepped back, knowing his gaze was all over her, kicked away her pants and her shoes.

Now she was naked, and the way he looked at her made her know she was beautiful in his eyes. She felt beautiful and not at all shy. She was his. All of her. Her hopes, her dreams, her body, her love.

He stood up, leaning a little, but not needing her to steady him, and he pushed his jeans and boxers down until he could shove them off to the side. Then he stood quite still, his arms at his sides, his back straight and tall.

She drank in the sight of him, the beauty of his chest with its dark swirls of hair, down to his flat stomach and hard thick manhood, and finally to his strong legs. She had never seen anyone so handsome before, so masculine. So ready.

Then her gaze moved to his hip, where she saw the scar, the reminder of the hell he'd been through. It didn't bother her. On the contrary, it made her long to hold him close, to reassure him that he was perfect just the way he was.

With him unmoving, watching her reaction, she reached over and ran her finger lightly over the ridge of reddened tissue. He flinched, but she knew she wasn't hurting him. Then she took his hand and brazenly brought it to her sex. Letting him feel how much she ached for him. Letting him see that the scar didn't matter.

His fingers slipped inside her and he groaned, ''Oh, Baby you're so wet. So hot.''

''Lie down,'' she whispered. ''Please.''

He obeyed, even though she could see he didn't want to stop touching her. He sat first, then lay back, shifting until his head was on his pillow.

She smiled as she lay down next to him. As she took him in her hand and felt him pulse with desire. He kissed her again, and she understood that he'd been holding back all this time. Waiting until he knew she accepted him.

He tried to move her to her back, but she stopped him. ''Not this time,'' she said. ''This time, it's my turn.''

''But—''

She kissed him silent as she pushed his shoulder back, then rose to her knees. She straddled him and rubbed against him until he begged her to stop. Then she guided him inside her, moving slowly, trembling as he filled her, as he made her complete.

She eased all the way down, making him gasp and reach for her. She put his hands on her breasts as she rode him. Slow and easy, squeezing him tight, abandoned to the flesh and the need, dizzy with a fulfillment she'd never dreamed of.

He caught her gaze and held it as she moved up and down, meeting his thrusts with thrusts of her own. Nothing in her life had prepared her for this. For this mixture of eroticism and love. For this perfect blend of heart, soul and body.

She wanted this forever. She wanted to wake up in this man's arms. To make love with him every night. To care for him and be cared for in return.

His hips moved faster, and his hand moved down her body until his thumb found her most sensitive spot. He rubbed in sensuous circles, bringing her closer and closer to completion.

It was too much. Suddenly she gasped and shuddered, every muscle in her body tightening and relaxing. She held on to him with her thighs, her hands on his chest, as he kept rubbing and rubbing until finally he cried out with his release.

She held him steady for a moment, then fell forward, laying her head on his shoulder, still trembling. "Jack," she whispered. "Oh, Jack."

He took in great breaths and hugged her. "I know, baby. I know."

"What have you done to me?" she asked.

His chuckle made his chest vibrate. "What have *I*

done? I swear, it's always the quiet ones you have to watch out for."

"Me?" she said. "Little old me?"

Jack lifted her head until he captured her gaze. He wanted to make sure she knew he was telling her the truth. "You. Only you."

She sighed, then laid her head on his chest. "That's lovely."

He wouldn't have chosen that word. He might have used *miraculous*. Because that was what it felt like. A miracle.

He'd never dared to believe this could happen. That she'd accept him so completely. That she'd give so much of herself.

He remembered when he'd first seen her hold Megan, how he'd thought he'd never feel that safe in a woman's arms. But tonight all that had changed.

He was home.

But it was a house of cards. Temporary at best. There wasn't enough to make it any more than that. "Hailey?"

"Huh?" She sounded sleepy. Which wasn't a bad thing. It made it easier to talk.

"You asked me once what had happened. About my hip."

She ran her hand across his chest and hugged him more tightly. "You don't need to tell me."

"I want to."

She kissed him on the shoulder, then relaxed again.

"I was on a stakeout about four months ago. Me and Frank. We were investigating a murder. We didn't have a lot to go on. The killer was clever, and he'd tried to make it look like the victim had killed herself. But we found some trace evidence. He was her boyfriend, and she had some money and a Mercedes she'd earmarked for him. He liked to gamble and he needed a way to pay some debts."

"Nice way to solve a problem," Hailey said.

"He was a swell guy. He made it look like she'd shot herself. And let me tell you, he did a hell of a job. Just not good enough. There were fibers."

"Fibers?"

"That's all it would take to bring him in. If we could make a match."

"And that's why you were watching him?"

"Yeah. He knew we were getting close and that the lab boys would nail him. We were making sure he didn't bolt before we got the evidence."

"He tried to get away?"

"Yep. And he had a small arsenal to help him. I saw the first two weapons. But not the third one."

"It must have been awful."

"We got him, but not until after…after he'd done his damage."

"After he'd turned your world upside down," she said softly, as if talking more to herself than him.

"I've never been anything but a cop," he said. "I went into the department right after college. I'd never wanted to do anything else. Not ever. I'm not sure why. I don't have any relatives in law enforcement."

"You're still a cop, Jack," she said. "The bullet didn't change that."

"Yes, it did. You know it did."

"Then you have to work hard to get well."

"Even if I do, there's no guarantee."

"You can't worry about that. You have to take one step at a time. Do the work and leave the results alone."

"I don't know if I can."

She sat up and so did he. She took his face in her hands. "Of course you can. You can do anything you set your mind on. And I'll help. I'll be right there with you, if you want me."

He wanted to say, *Sure. Let's do it for the Gipper. You and me, babe, against the world.* But that would be a lie. "I didn't tell you this to ask for help."

"I know that," she said, dropping her hands. Her enthusiasm of a second ago diminished.

"No, I don't think you do. I told you that so you'll understand why this can't go any further."

She looked away for a moment, and when she looked back, her face was flushed with anger. "I don't recall asking for anything more."

"I know. You didn't. But I need you to be clear."

"I'm perfectly clear. And perfectly furious that you had to go and spoil something perfectly wonderful."

"I didn't mean to spoil anything."

"But you did, you big jerk. You're so damn worried about tomorrow that you can't enjoy today. Well, we might not get a tomorrow, who knows? Or we may see a hundred tomorrows. It doesn't matter, because the only thing real is right now. You and me, in this bed, in this house. What's real is how you made me feel. And how I made you feel."

He looked at her for a long time, at her determination and her righteous anger. And then he laughed. Hard.

"What's so funny?" she asked.

"I am a big jerk," he said. "A colossal jackass."

"Damn straight," she said. And then he saw her lip curve up, just a hair.

He took her hands and pulled her to him. "Can you forgive me?"

"No," she said. "Never."

"Never's a long time."

"I don't have any other plans."

"How about if I give you something else to think about? Something distracting?"

"I'm sorry," she said. "There's nothing you can do that will make me change my mind."

"How about this?" he asked, moving his hand down below the comforter.

Her eyes widened as he touched her. "Oh, okay. You're right. That'll work."

He laughed again, but only for a moment. Only until he kissed her.

Chapter Sixteen

Jack woke up with a start. Something had pulled him from sleep, but he couldn't put his finger on it. Certainly it wasn't the woman sleeping in his arms.

He looked at her and was amazed at how much he cared about her. She'd opened a door he hadn't even known existed. She'd shown him he did have a heart. A heart that could love, and could break.

God, she was beautiful! Her blond hair was tousled. Her skin was smooth and luminous. Her eyelashes, resting on her perfect cheeks, captivated him for several moments.

It still amazed him that she hadn't minded his scar. That she hadn't minded that he was no acrobat in bed. All she'd done was love him senseless. He could barely believe it, even with the proof lying right next to him.

He turned carefully to look at the clock. It was early, just after six. What had woken him? What was still scratching at the door of his consciousness?

Something about Frank. That was it. Something about what had happened yesterday. But what?

Maybe it was being shot at. It had probably brought up some memories of when he'd been wounded. That seemed logical, but…

He'd go wash up. Shave. Think of something else. Think of Hailey.

It took him longer than usual to get out of bed, not just because he didn't want to disturb her, but because his cane was in the other room. He used the bedside table to stand and then gritted his teeth for the walk to the bathroom, stopping briefly to put on the robe Hailey had lent him.

To his surprise, the walk wasn't that bad. It wasn't great, but he could handle it. Could the exercises have worked so quickly? Or was it just the natural healing process? He didn't care. All he knew was that it was a good sign. The first ray of light he'd seen since the night he'd been shot.

No, that wasn't true. Hailey had taken him out of the darkness. Megan, too.

He thought about the woman and the little girl as he went about his morning routine. It struck him that he was humming. An old Glen Campbell song. ''Galveston.'' He hadn't heard the song in years. He hadn't hummed in… He'd never hummed.

He concentrated on shaving without butchering his face, and then he saw a beautiful woman appear in the mirror. Hailey.

''Good morning,'' she said, her voice still husky with sleep.

''Did I wake you?''

She shook her head.

''I'll be done in a second.''

"Don't rush on my account." She sat on the edge of the bathtub, her pink bathrobe falling open to reveal her legs. He made the mistake of looking. The sight of her legs had him wanting her again. He stirred, wondering if he could ask her to put off her shower for about an hour.

She was looking at her feet. Rocking gently back and forth. She must have heard him humming a minute ago, because now she was softly humming the same tune.

Then it hit him. He dropped his razor and gripped the sides of the sink before he fell. *Galveston.* He hadn't caught it yesterday. It had slipped right by him.

"Jack?" Hailey said, suddenly at his side. "What's wrong? Is it your hip?"

He shook his head. "No."

"What? You look as white as the shaving cream."

He got a towel from the rod and wiped his face, replaying in his head the conversation with Frank word for word.

"Tell me!"

He swallowed, then faced her. "Yesterday, after the gunshot..."

"Yes?"

"Frank told me to go home. That it would take me two hours to get here."

She nodded, not getting it.

"I never told him we were in Galveston. I never told anyone. But he said the ferry would be murder. How'd he know that?"

Her face changed from confusion to fear. "He

might not have meant anything by that, Jack. It might have been just an assumption.''

''What if it wasn't? No, no. You're right. Not Frank. He wouldn't do anything like that. He's a straight-up guy. He'd never do anything illegal, and he'd sure as hell never do anything to hurt me.''

''Right,'' she said. ''It was a misunderstanding. You're just worried, that's all.''

''Yeah,'' he said, not really believing it.

''Maybe you slipped and told him on the phone?''

He shook his head. ''I didn't. There's no way he could know we were here. I never said a word.''

''I can't believe it,'' she said, shaking her head. ''It just doesn't feel right.''

''When does betrayal feel right?'' He put the towel back on the rod. ''Why don't you take your shower?'' he said. ''Then I think you'd better pack.''

''Really?''

He nodded. ''It's not safe here, Hailey.''

''Where will we go?''

''We'll figure it out later. Now go on. Get ready. I'll put some coffee on. You take care of Megan.''

She touched his arm, then kissed him on the cheek. ''We'll get through this,'' she whispered. ''Together.''

He nodded, then left for the kitchen. It was all he could do to make it to his cane. His hip hurt like hell.

HAILEY WORKED QUICKLY, trying not to panic and not to frighten Megan. She threw her things into her suitcase and then borrowed one from her mother's closet for Megan's things. By the time she was finished, Jack's duffel bag was packed and ready in the living room, and Megan was busy drawing at the kitchen table.

So intent was she that her little tongue stuck out, just the tip, as she scribbled furiously. Hailey felt the familiar tug that had already become a part of her. The love she felt was deeper than a few days. It was a lifetime kind of love. And with it came the need to protect her. To keep her safe.

Then she looked at Jack. He was so despondent she ached for him. There had to be *something* they could do.

She'd thought about it all morning, and she knew Jack was thinking about it, too. Only one idea had come to her, but she was afraid he wouldn't go for it. And if he didn't?

No, she'd make him see that it was their only chance. She walked over to him, out of Megan's hearing range. He took her hand and kissed her palm. "I'm sorry," he whispered.

"About what?"

"Today shouldn't have been about this," he said.

"I'll get over it."

He sighed as he looked at her deeply, as his troubled gaze searched her face. "It's no good," he said. "I don't think we should use the computer. For all we know they've already figured out a way to hack in to your mailbox. And I don't think I should call Frank." He closed his eyes for a second, then looked at her again. "And I can't call Bob, because I can't trust a living soul except you."

She leaned over and kissed him gently on the mouth, then moved back to present her idea. "I was thinking..." she said.

"About?"

"About what we can do."

"I'm all ears."

"I think we should go to Faraday's office. To-night, late."

"You mean break in?"

She nodded. "What we need is some kind of tie between the names those initials might represent and Faraday. We need a connection there, and we need some kind of proof that the numbers are what we think they are, right?"

"Yeah, but we're not going to get it by breaking into his office. And even if we could get the evidence we needed, I'm in no shape to take any risks."

"I know," she said. "That's why *I'm* going to do it."

His incredulity made his mouth open as he tried to form words. Finally he gathered himself together enough to say, "No. No way in hell. No."

"Tell me how you really feel," she joked. But he wasn't in a joking mood.

"It's not going to happen," he said. "And that's final."

She didn't react to his edict. She'd been prepared for it. "Here's what I figure," she said. "We have to get out of here. We have no place to go. No place safe. Except I know a shop downtown. I've actually been there with one of my web-site clients. It's like a spy-supply store. They have little microphones and cameras, everything we'd need."

He opened his mouth to argue, but she put her hand on his lips.

"We'll be in contact every second. I'll get in and get out. No one will be the wiser."

"How will you get in?"

"You'll help me."

"And what about security? Cameras, alarms?"

"We'll be cautious. If something goes wrong, I'll leave. I'll be out of there in a heartbeat."

"No," he said, his voice and demeanor immovable.

"Jack, we know we can't stay here. They'll come for us. We can't go home and we can't ask for help. They're going to get Megan if we don't do something."

"Not this."

"Then what?"

"I can't let you do this. I won't."

"I won't be alone. You'll be with me every step of the way. I'll just be your legs, that's all. And if you say to get out, I will."

"What about her?" he asked, nodding at Megan.

"I've thought about that, too. Do you think your ex would look after her?"

He laughed. "Crystal? Baby-sit? She gets hives around kids."

"You could ask her."

"Okay, let's assume she says yes. That we go to this store and outfit ourselves like James Bond. That you manage to get into Faraday's office. What are you going to do if someone shows up? If you're trapped, I can't come get you. Do you understand? I won't be able to help if something goes wrong.''

She nodded. ''I know. And I'm willing to take that risk.''

''Why?''

''Because I can't live knowing that someone wants to hurt Megan. Because I can't stand the thought of someone hurting you. I'd rather die than see either of you in pain.''

''What happens to me if it's you who——''

''I'll be fine. I promise. If it looks at all like I'll get caught, I'm out of there. I'm not doing this to prove anything, Jack. I'm doing it because we have no other choice.''

He didn't answer. He stared at Megan for a long time. He flinched, and she knew he was thinking about Frank. Then he turned back to her. ''It's all gone,'' he said. ''Everything I ever counted on.''

''No,'' she said. ''It's different. Not gone.''

''I'm a cripple, Hailey. I can do exercises from here to the next millennium, but I'm never going to be whole again.''

''You think that because you limp, you're not whole? You're the most complete man I've ever met, Jack McCabe. You're thoughtful and strong and funny and smart. You're kind and you're sexy. I can see why Crystal loved you.''

He looked at her as if he thought she was crazy. She wondered if she should say more, but the dismissal in his gaze told her no.

''Haven't you been paying attention? I have nothing. I told you. All I've ever been is a cop, and now I'm not a cop anymore. All I could ever count on was my training, and a bullet took care of that. I have nothing to offer you. Nothing.''

''You have your mind and you have your courage. So as far as I can see, you have the whole world at your feet. There's nothing you can't do.''

He shook his head, then turned away. He swallowed twice, then cleared his throat. When he turned back, his eyes glistened with tears. ''I want to believe you.''

''Then believe me.''

''I don't know if I can.''

She kissed him again. ''You can. You just have to want to.'' She stood up and went over to Megan. ''Guess what?'' she said, her voice high and light. ''We're going to go see that nice lady friend of Jack's,'' she said. ''As soon as he makes a phone call.''

She picked Megan up and felt the little girl's arms wrap around her neck. Of course she could do this. She could fight armies and win. Because she was doing it for Megan. And for her only chance at happiness.

He shook his head. ''No. I mean it. No.''

''Jack, I mean it, too. I'm doing this. Alone if I have to. So you might as well get on with it.''

He went to the phone, his limp more exaggerated than it had been in days. He dialed, then waited a moment. Then he said, ''Crystal? I've got another favor to ask.''

''Gee, what a surprise.''

"Look, this is important, or I wouldn't ask you."

He heard her sigh. She'd give him hell about this. She had some excellent points, Crystal, but she couldn't hold a candle to Hailey.

"What is it?" she asked grudgingly.

"I need you to watch the kid. Just for tonight."

She burst out laughing. "Me? Baby-sit?"

"Yeah, you."

"Frank said you were going off the deep end. Now I know he's right."

Jack's heart practically stopped beating. "You've been talking to Frank?"

"Yeah."

"Did you tell him that I'm with Hailey and Megan?"

"No."

He breathed again.

"He told me."

Dammit. That's how come they'd gotten so close. Frank must have traced him through the Cadillac. Followed him to Galveston. It made real sense now, even though it was still so hard to believe the Frank he knew could be working for someone like Faraday.

"Are you still there?" Crystal asked.

"Yeah. We'll bring Megan over in an hour or so. She's a good kid. You'll like her. And Crystal?"

"Yeah?"

"Do me a favor and don't talk to Frank anymore. At least, not for awhile."

"I assume you'll tell me why."

"When it's over. Then I'll tell you everything."

JACK DIDN'T LIKE IT. He didn't like any part of it. But nothing he'd said so far had dissuaded Hailey from this crazy scheme of hers.

They'd reached Faraday's offices just after one in the morning, and now he was driving slowly around the perimeter, trying to get a feel for the layout and to check out the security measures. At the front of the building he saw a night watchman sitting behind a counter. For some reason, probably the dark street and the brilliant light in the window, it reminded him of that painting *Nighthawks*.

Hailey sighed. "I didn't think there'd be an all-night guard."

"So, you happy now? You ready to give it up?"

"Is there an alternative? Apart from leaving the state and changing our names? But then, that didn't work for Roy, did it?"

Jack cursed and she slugged him in the shoulder.

"Good thing Megan isn't here," she muttered.

"The kid's gotta learn some time. Hell, she's getting an education with Crystal, you can count on that."

Hailey's brow furrowed. "Jack, it's a little late to tell me the woman is dangerous, don't you think?"

He patted her knee. "Don't worry. Megan will be fine. Confused, but fine."

"Okay, then. I'll just have to get past the guard, won't I?"

"And how do you propose to do that?"

"I'm not sure."

"And if he has cameras in the hall? He'll get a

real nice picture of you breaking in. It'll probably be on the front page of tomorrow's paper.''

"I'll find out if he has cameras, and if he does, I'll find out if they show the hallways. Sometimes they don't.''

"This is insane,'' Jack said, pulling the car to the curb at the side of the building. "Hailey, I can't let you do this. There are a million reasons you shouldn't even try.''

"But one very compelling reason I have to.''

"I can't be Megan's mother if something happens to you,'' he said, knowing he was hitting below the belt.

She winced. "You won't have to be. As long as we keep the lines of communication open, everything will be fine.''

"And if we don't?''

"I'll get out of there so fast it'll make your head spin.''

"It's already spinning. Dammit, Hailey, I can't do this.''

"Sure you can. You will.''

"Why?'' he asked, grateful for the lamppost on the street. He could see her face, see her incredible eyes. Of course, he could also see her determination.

She leaned over and kissed him, and not just a quick buss. It was a kiss that made him remember every detail of last night. Their first night together. Probably their last. When she pulled back, her hand lingered on his cheek. "You will because you care about me,'' she whispered.

"I do?''

She nodded. "Don't panic. I know you haven't gotten that far yet. But I certainly intend to be there when you do."

"I don't want to lose you. You're the only thing in my life that makes any sense. Except for this part," he said.

"This part does, too. I'm going to do this right, Jack. You'll just have to trust me and believe my instincts are good."

She kissed him again. A long hard kiss that made him pray the night watchman would throw her out on her beautiful behind.

It was just after two when she slipped from his hold. He checked his watch twice. "If you're not out of there in half an hour, I'm calling the cavalry."

"I can't do anything in half an hour. But I'll be back by four-fifteen." She got out of the car. "Put on your thingy," she said before slamming the heavy door.

He smiled. But he knew what she meant. He slipped on the earphones and turned on the transmitter. Meanwhile she put her little earpiece in and then double-checked her wire. Then she walked down the street. "Can you hear me?"

He winced. "You don't have to shout."

"Is this better?"

"Yes. Just talk in a normal tone of voice."

"Can you tell I'm shaking in my boots?"

He could tell her to come back now, to stop this before it got out of hand. But she wouldn't. She'd go on without his support. Without his voice in her ear. "You sound fine. Like you do this for a living."

She started across the street. "Wish me luck."

"Come back to me," he said right into his mike. "That's all I ask. I don't want to go on without you."

"You won't have to. I promise."

"If anything feels weird, don't hesitate. Just get out."

"Jack?"

"What?"

"Shut up. I'm going inside."

His adrenaline spiked, and he wondered if he was going to have a heart attack before she got past the watchman. Wouldn't *that* be nice.

Dammit to hell, why was he so useless? He hit his hip, wincing at the very overt reminder that he wasn't worth a damn anymore. He was letting a woman do his dirty work for him. *His* woman.

If there was a lower feeling in the world, he didn't want to know about it.

Then he heard her voice. Or what he assumed was her voice. She sounded more like Crystal. Low and sexy, her voice was like slow-flowing molasses. And her story, jeez. Something about a diamond necklace and a reward and Craig Faraday's wife.

Jack had to smile. He could hear her beguiling the night watchman. Sucking him in. She couldn't have done this a couple of weeks ago. The woman he'd met that first day wouldn't have had it in her. But since then, she'd saved two lives. Megan's and his. She'd given them shelter. She'd made them forget that the world was a damn harsh place.

If anyone could get past that guard, it was her.

"Oh, thank you so much," he heard her say.

He must have missed the denouement. The moment the guard surrendered.

But he heard her walking now, her heels clicking on the hard floor. And a heavier tread.

"Thank you so much, Darrel," Hailey said again in his earphones. "I can't believe how foolish I've been. I promise, I won't be in there more than five minutes."

She'd been right about the dress, hadn't she? He'd told her to wear black. Pants, shirt, everything. She'd come out in black, all right. A black dress that fit her like a second skin.

The ding of the elevator sounded, but he didn't hear footsteps. Carpet, that had to be why. He turned up the volume, dying to know what was happening. Nothing, and then, "No, no. Please don't bother. I know you must have a great deal of work to do. I'll just be a few minutes, and then I'll come down and sign out."

Jack couldn't believe it. She'd gotten the guard to open the door for her.

"Jack?"

He lifted the mike to his mouth. "Yeah?"

"I'm inside."

"I know."

"I'm going to look in Faraday's desk."

"Hurry."

"Trust me. I will. But, Jack?"

"Uh-huh?"

"I was right about the dress."

"I'll congratulate you properly when you get out of there."

"Ah, incentives," she said. "I like that."

"Stop talking and hurry up."

"Oh, God. I'm scared to death."

"I'm right across from the parking lot," he said. "I can see the front entrance, too. If anyone goes in, I'll tell you."

"Okay. But, Jack?"

He shook his head, but then he heard a drawer open. So she wasn't just standing at the door talking to him. Good girl. "Yes?"

"There's something I forgot to tell you."

"What?"

"I'm in love with you."

Chapter Seventeen

Hailey was shaking so hard it was difficult to use her hands. She had lucked out so far, but with every second that went by she felt more and more afraid. What if the guard had just acted nice, but then called Faraday? Or the police?

"Jack?"

"Yes."

"Don't you have anything you want to say to me?"

"I do, but I don't want to say it over a microphone."

"This desk drawer is locked," she said.

He closed his eyes, debating whether to lie to her and tell her Faraday was entering the building. No. She was already inside. If she could get the proof they needed, it would change everything for her and Megan. And for him. But dammit to hell, he never wanted to feel this helpless again. "Use the lock pick I showed you how to use."

"On the desk?"

"It's the same principle."

''Okay, hold on.''

He listened more intently than ever before in his life. Every scrape, click and bang felt like a physical blow. Her breathing was louder now, too, telling him she was struggling. If he'd been up there, that drawer would have been open in seconds. But he'd never have gotten past the guard.

A light from behind startled him. Headlights from a slow-moving car. He lowered the volume on the transmitter in case it was the police. Sure enough, the blue car was a Houston PD vehicle, and any second now they were going to find him behind the wheel. That wasn't so bad, except that it was Crystal's car. If they were on the ball, they'd do some checking. And if they did some checking, they might find Megan.

The police pulled up right next to him and shone a bright beam of light at him. He put his hand up to shade his eyes. ''Hey, knock it off,'' he said. ''I'm a cop.''

The light moved down and out of his eyes. ''Oh, yeah?'' came a deep voice.

''Yeah. I'm Detective Jack McCabe. I've got my ID right here.''

''Yeah, yeah, I've seen you before,'' came a higher voice, the driver's. ''You're that officer who got shot a few months ago.''

''That's me,'' he said, his vision slowly coming back so he could make out the two men in the car. He didn't recognize either of them.

''So what are you doing out here so late?'' the second cop asked.

"A favor for a dizzy dame friend of mine. She left something important up in her office. And she won't go to bed until she gets it."

The cop chuckled. "Dames, huh?"

"Yeah. Can't live with 'em—" Jack began.

"Can't lock 'em up without a warrant," the young cop finished.

Jack laughed, hoping the car and its occupants would move on, willing it with all his power.

"You take care, Detective."

It worked. Or maybe they'd just finished with him. "'Night," he said, nodding. He didn't give a damn why they were leaving, just that they were. And that they weren't on Faraday's payroll. He'd know that soon enough.

When they were all the way down the block and turning the corner, Jack increased the volume on the transmitter.

"Where are you! Jack!"

"I'm here. It's okay."

She sighed, her voice so shaky he thought she might be crying. "What happened?"

"A police car came by. But they've already left, none the wiser." He made it sound easy, as if he didn't have any worries about them coming back. Coming back with friends.

"Oh, my God, you nearly gave me a heart attack. Did you hear anything I said?"

"No."

"I got the drawer open. There's a bunch of numbered computer disks in here. Which might be something. But there's also a couple of telephone logs, you know, the pink ones that are used to record calls?''

''Yeah, I know what they are.''

''Well, guess what. I see a whole bunch of initials. Initials we've both seen before.''

''So take them and get the hell out.''

''What about the disks?''

''Take those, too. But hurry. Hailey, get out of there.'' He heard the sound of disks rubbing together and a soft curse, which surprised him. Then the sound of a drawer closing.

''Okay,'' she said.

''Now!''

''I'm coming,'' she said. ''We did— Oh!''

''What is it?'' he yelled, his blood growing cold at the sound of her gasp. ''Hailey! Hailey!''

''Why don't you put the purse down, miss.''

It was a male voice. Not the voice of the guard, either.

''You don't have to point that gun at me,'' Hailey said. ''I'm not going to argue.''

''That's right, you're not. Go on, get over there.''

Jack whipped out Hailey's cellular phone and dialed 911. He reported a heart attack at Faraday's office. He gave a phony name. Then he called Bob. Even though it was a risk, it was a risk he'd have to take. Bob answered groggily. ''Yeah?''

''It's me,'' he said. ''I need help.''

''What?''

''Get over to Faraday's office. It's the building on Fourteenth and Alabama. Fourth floor. I'm in trouble.''

"I'm on my way."

"And, Bob!"

"Yeah?"

"Don't tell Frank."

There were a few seconds of silence. "I won't."

Jack clicked the off button and turned his entire attention to Hailey. He didn't know what he'd missed during his phone calls, but at least she was still talking. There hadn't been any gunshots.

"I do know you," she said. "You're the detective I met at Roy Chandler's apartment."

Damn. She was in so much trouble. Jack brought the microphone close to his lips. "Hang on, baby. Help is on the way. You just stall him. Don't do anything funny. I'm right here with you every step of the way."

"What's this? What were you planning to do with these?" the man asked roughly. "Huh? That's breaking and entering, larceny. Hell, little gal, I've got you on so much you aren't ever gonna get out of prison."

"Don't listen to him, Hailey. He's not a cop. He's a phony. Just cooperate with him. Help is coming."

"Or maybe I should just shoot you right here. Save the taxpayers some money."

Jack pushed open the car door and got out his gun. The problem was the transmitter. If he took that, he couldn't use his cane. Or he'd have to put his gun away. The only thing he could do was forget the friggin' cane.

He shut the door behind him and started across the street. Each step felt like a hot knife sinking into his flesh. He concentrated on Hailey. On listening to the conversation upstairs.

"You just sit right down, honey," the man said. "And don't let me see your hands move from the top of your head."

"All right," she said, so calmly, God bless her, that she could have convinced a bonfire to go out on its own.

"Hailey," he said, "honey, listen to me. I'm coming, baby. I'm coming to get you. You just stay cool for a little while longer."

He heard a soft whimper, as if she was holding back a cry.

"And, honey? I love you, too. I do. I don't need any more time to figure it out. I know it. I've known it for days." He got to the front of the office building and tried to move faster so he could get inside. He took a wrong step and he almost fell, but he didn't. He just gritted his teeth and kept on moving.

"You're the only thing that matters to me, Hailey, so you can't do anything wrong. I never should have let you go up there. I don't want to live without you."

Again he heard the whimper.

"When I get up there, what we're going to do is make an offer. We're going to give them the damn ledger, okay? We'll give them anything they want, as long as they let you go. As long as they leave Megan alone. Nothing is more important than you, do you hear me?"

"Hey!" The phony cop's voice cut in. "What the—"

Silence. Nothing, not a sigh, not a breath, not a whimper. "Hailey!" he yelled into the microphone. "Hailey!" But she didn't answer.

The bastard had seen her wire. Now he knew she had an accomplice. And that she'd probably signaled for help. Which meant he might just kill her and leave. Or take her with him. Or, oh, God, he didn't know, but he had to get to her. If he had to climb the building by himself, he'd get to her.

He pulled open the glass door, scaring the night watchman so badly he almost fell off his stool.

"Hey!"

Jack headed right for the elevator. "I'm a cop. More cops are coming. Tell them I'm in Faraday's office." Then he pushed the button again and again, wishing he could take the stairs. Wishing he'd never let her go.

"I'm calling the police!" the guard shouted.

"I already did, but be my guest," Jack said. And then the elevator arrived. He lurched inside and pushed the button for the fourth floor. The elevator seemed to take forever. Jack got ready to go, clicking the safety off his gun, leaning on his good leg, taking calming breaths just as Hailey had taught him.

And then the doors opened—at the third floor. He hit the fourth-floor button again, but now it wouldn't stay lit.

The guard! The guard had stopped the elevator, and Hailey was up there alone.

He banged his fist on the wall. Hard. And then he got moving. He needed to find the staircase, and fast.

HAILEY STUDIED THE MAN with the gun as if her life depended on it. He wasn't bright, but then she'd known that when she'd seen him at Roy's apartment. But that just made him more likely to shoot first and ask questions later.

Her best bet was to keep on playing the innocent miss. A smarter man would have made the connection that a person who's just broken into an office and taken private disks from a locked drawer probably didn't get there by mistake.

But her biggest worry wasn't the hulking man going through her purse. It was Jack. He was sure to be thinking the worst now that their communication was cut off. And knowing Jack, she was positive he was coming after her.

Which made it twice as hard to be still, to act calm. She'd never meant to put Jack's life in danger. She'd actually never thought her own life would be in danger. What would Megan do without either of them? She blinked back tears. This was no time to fall apart.

JACK LOOKED UP the long staircase. It seemed like Everest to him. A torturous journey that would go on forever. Even with his cane, it would have been too much for him.

But the thought of Hailey gave him the courage to take the first step. He gasped with the pain, clutching his hip. *Hailey.* He took another step. And another. By the time he was halfway up, he was sweating. His legs were shaking, the muscles in his thighs trembling with the effort of carrying him. He wouldn't let the pain win. *Hailey*.

Finally he made it to the landing. He turned and moaned. There was yet another set of stairs, this one not as long as the one he'd just climbed, but even a curb would hurt him now. But he had to keep going. Putting one foot up a stair, holding on to the rail, then dragging the other foot up to the same stair. Then doing it again and again, until he thought his hip would give out.

It didn't. He made it to the fourth-floor door. He needed a moment to catch his breath, and as he gulped in oxygen, he thought about *before*. Before, he would have climbed this stupid staircase in two seconds, three steps at a time. No. Before, he wouldn't have had to go after Hailey, because he'd have gone himself.

Which is what he should have done, anyway. He should have gone, despite his injury. Despite everything. He'd been a fool. He'd let Frank's betrayal get to him. He'd felt sorry for himself, and now look what had happened. He'd put her in harm's way. The one person who mattered. The woman he loved, and he'd put her in danger.

The agony of his thoughts was worse than the pain in his hip. He opened the door slowly, listening. He didn't hear anything at all.

Holding his breath, he stepped into the corridor. It was empty. A sign on the wall told him Faraday's office was to his right. He headed that way, holding his pistol steady. Fighting the urge to cry out as he supported himself on his bad leg.

Just as he reached the men's-room door, he heard the elevator ding. Someone was here. Either it was Bob or the fire department or one of Faraday's men.

He pushed himself into the men's room, grateful it wasn't locked. It was very dark, and he didn't turn on the light. Instead, he opened the door a sliver. He couldn't see the corridor, but he could hear.

Footsteps. It sounded like one person. Whoever it was passed the washroom, then Jack couldn't hear anything more. He must have gone inside. There might be someone else stationed at the elevator door. Jack would have to risk it.

He stepped out slowly, leading with his gun. But there was no one by the elevator. Moving as quickly as he could, he continued down the hall to Faraday's office. Just as he reached the door, he heard Bob Dorran's voice. Thank God.

But the words, they weren't right.

"He's sitting in a Cadillac, around the corner. He's crippled, but he can still use his gun. Keep quiet—don't tip him off. Then kill him."

Jack lurched backward, almost falling. Bob? His best friend? The betrayal rocked him. He wanted to march into the room and confront Bob, but now wasn't the time. He had to be invisible while Bob's partner went out. The reception desk! He dived straight for it, praying his gun wouldn't go off. That he'd be able to hide before he made the gunman's job that much easier.

He fell on his shoulder and a white-hot knife of pain sliced through him. Biting his lip, he crawled forward, listening as footsteps grew nearer and nearer.

A second after he got his bad leg behind the desk, Nichols walked past him and went out the door. Jack didn't breathe for another minute, just in case the guy came back for something.

He didn't. But he would be back when he discovered his target had fled the Cadillac. There wasn't much time. Where the hell was the fire department? How could he get to Dorran and make sure Hailey didn't get shot in the process?

"I THOUGHT YOU WERE Jack's friend," Hailey said. "I thought you cared about him."

"I did," Dorran said. "But he should have minded his own business."

"Does Frank know? Or is he in this with you?"

"Frank? He doesn't know squat. Especially now."

Hailey shivered at his tone. At his appearance. He looked like a desperate man, with his hair plastered to his head with his own sweat, his stained polo shirt sticking to him in patches on his chest and arms. He'd forgotten to zip his fly all the way, although he'd remembered to wear underwear.

He'd clearly thrown his clothes on and raced here, intent on killing Jack. On killing her. But only after he got what he wanted.

"So where is it?"

"I can't tell you that."

He moved closer to her chair and she flinched. Her arms were killing her, and more than anything she wanted to lower them and rest. But her instructions had been clear. She wasn't willing to die over sore arms.

"You think I don't know about the kid? That Barry gave the book to her?"

"You're wrong. She doesn't have it. She's completely innocent. For God's sake, she's only four."

"Look at me," he said. "Look at me!"

She forced herself to stare into his dark manic eyes.

"Do I seem like the kind of man who'd hesitate to kill a kid?"

Hailey had to look away, because the answer was no. A stunning awful no. He wouldn't think twice about hurting Megan.

Oh, God. What had she done? She should have listened to Jack. He'd been right all along. She'd forced him into this terrible mess, without giving him any options, any leeway.

She was, in effect, killing them both. Killing the two people she loved most in the world. All because she was stubborn. Because she thought she could do anything. That she'd changed, that Jack's love had made her strong, invulnerable.

Being wrong shouldn't have these kinds of consequences. But they did.

The minute she told Dorran where the book was, she was dead. But if she delayed much longer, she'd be dead, too.

"I'm getting tired of this bull." He lunged at her, lifting her from her chair by the front of her dress, hurting her, terrifying her. "You tell me or so help me God I'll make you wish you were dead."

She turned away from his horrible breath and his horrible words. She didn't know what to do. *Jack, Jack, please. Help me.*

And then, because there was mercy and goodness left in the world, she saw him. She saw Jack creeping up to Bob Dorran. She saw the man she loved coming to rescue her, even when she didn't deserve to be rescued.

He held his finger to his lips, then lifted his knee, mimicking a groin kick. Then he held up three fingers, telling her to wait for the count before acting. He moved closer, limping badly. Where was his cane?

Dorran must have seen her react to Jack. He tightened his grip on her and started to turn.

Jack wasn't close enough.

Chapter Eighteen

Jack saw Dorran turn and for a moment he thought it was all over. That Dorran was going to pull the trigger and kill Hailey. But instead of keeping his weapon trained on her, he swung it at him.

Jack's instincts kicked in. He signaled Hailey to use her knee at the exact time he charged Bob. As if making a football tackle, he used his shoulder to bash into Dorran's side a split second after he heard a yell that could only mean Hailey had connected. "Get out of here!" he screamed, going for Dorran's gun, which lay just to the right of the man's outstretched arm.

Jack crawled desperately as Dorran lurched for the weapon, but Hailey must have gotten him good, because he didn't move very quickly.

Just quickly enough to win.

As Jack tried to aim his own gun, he saw Hailey's high heel come down hard on Dorran's hand. Even Jack winced as Dorran screamed again. Then Hailey bent down, picked up the gun and held her other hand out for Jack.

Another time, another life, he would have been embarrassed to have her help him up. Humiliated to have her be the one to get the gun. But now, he put his hand in hers gratefully and, with her strength and his determination, stood up.

She smiled, although he could see she was still terrified. Then she handed him the gun. He kissed her on the forehead, and then he concentrated on Bob Dorran. One of his oldest friends. A guy he'd have taken a bullet for. Whom he'd trusted with his life. "Was it so much money?" he asked.

Dorran didn't look at him. He curled his legs up to his chest and moaned over his limp and broken hand.

Hailey touched Jack's free arm. "He said something about Frank. I think he's in trouble."

"You mean Frank's not in on it?"

Hailey shook her head.

"Can you make a few phone calls?"

She nodded.

"Call 911 and tell them there's an injury at Frank's house." He gave her the address, and she wrote it down with very shaky fingers. "Then call Sergeant Bittner at the police department. Tell him Nichols is by the car—that I said he needs to be taken in. And call the FBI and tell them to get out here."

Just as she picked up the phone, the door behind them burst open, and Jack spun around, prepared to shoot Nichols on the spot. But it was the paramedics, who froze the instant they saw the gun.

He quickly held up his hand. "I'm Detective Jack

McCabe," he said. "HPD. This man is under a
and he's wounded."

The young paramedics, one with shocking red
hair, looked at each other, then got to work. As they
checked on Dorran's wounds, Jack read him his
rights. Dorran didn't say boo. He just cried like a
child. No. Megan would have had more dignity than
that.

"I spoke to the sergeant. He's going to help get
Nichols and alert the FBI," Hailey said. "And someone's going to Frank's house."

For the first time since this night had begun, he let
himself relax. Not much, but enough to pull her to
his side and give her the kind of kiss she deserved.
She felt so damn good in his arms. So right.

"Where's your cane?" she asked after a moment.

"I couldn't bring it," he said. "Needed my hands
free. Good thing we've been doing those exercises,
huh?"

She shook her head, frowning. "You've probably
hurt yourself all over again. Why don't we have these
nice men take a look at you?"

"No. Not tonight. I'll go see the doc tomorrow if
I need to."

"You need to."

"Yes, dear," he said, amazed at her concern over
him. Amazed that he'd cared more about her life than
his own. "Are you all right?"

She nodded. "Fine, except for the adrenaline. I
feel like I could run a two-minute mile."

"That'll pass. Eventually."

The paramedics lifted Bob onto the gurney.

n to Ben Taub Hospital,'' the one
old him. "If he's under arrest, we

lailey, not wanting to leave her.

It's okay,'' she said. "I'll talk to the FBI. I know
as much as you do.''

"Fine,'' he said, "but we're not leaving until
Nichols is captured.''

She looked at him, then at the paramedics and the
now silent Bob Dorran. "Can we wait in the other
room?''

Jack turned to the redhead. "You got cuffs?''

He nodded. He went into his medical kit and
pulled out a pair, then Jack did the honors. He
hooked Dorran's good arm to the gurney. "The kid
didn't know anything,'' he said to him. "She was
four, for God's sake. What did you expect from
her?''

Dorran didn't answer. He didn't even look at him.

"I'm gonna make sure you go down hard for
this,'' Jack said. "You and Faraday and everyone in
the department who's in on this.'' Then he turned
and limped over to Hailey. "Mind giving me a shoulder to lean on?'' he asked.

She smiled up at him as she put his arm around
her. "We're a team, aren't we?''

"Yeah,'' he agreed. Together they made it into
Faraday's office, then to his desk, where Jack leaned
against it so the pressure was off his leg.

He drew her close and kissed her again. She kissed
him back, and for a long stretch that's all they did.

But finally she pulled away just enough to talk to him.

"I'm sorry," she said. "I never should have forced you into this."

"Are you kidding? I was the one who shouldn't have let you go."

"But it turned out all right, didn't it? I mean, it was scary there for a while, but now Megan will be safe and we can go back to our lives."

"I don't want to go back," he said.

"No?"

He shook his head slowly, keeping his gaze locked on hers. "I never did much care for that life. I'm thinking about starting a new one."

"It's a little late for you to run off and join the circus," she said.

"Damn. I guess that means I only have one option left."

"And what would that be?"

"Marrying you."

She sighed happily. "It's not just me, you know."

He nodded. "Megan's included in the deal."

"What about all your concerns?"

"I've still got plenty. But now, see, I have a partner. And together we do okay. I'm thinking there are several options. Private-investigation work if it doesn't work out with the department, but I think it will. Who knows, if we keep doing those damn exercises, I might just be able to get my old job back."

"Jack?"

"Yeah?"

"Did you mean it? What you said before?"

He kissed her on the nose. "Every word."

"I'm glad," she said. Then she leaned over to kiss him back, but she pressed too hard on his hip and he grimaced. "Are you okay?"

"Fine. Except for hurting like hell. But that doesn't matter."

"It matters to me. Everything about you matters to me."

"I know," he said. "And that's what makes it all right. That's what makes it all worth it."

A knock on the door startled them both. Hailey turned just as a man with an FBI badge walked into the room.

Jack didn't see her again for more than twelve hours. He didn't stop thinking about her for a minute.

Epilogue

Hailey looked deeply into Jack's eyes as the judge said the words that made them husband and wife. What she saw there was more than love, although love would have been enough. She saw admiration, strength, courage and the humor that let her know that laughter would be part of their marriage.

They leaned in together, meeting in the middle for the kiss that sealed the deal. The beautiful kiss that represented the happiest moment of her life.

When they pulled apart, he caught her gaze. "Hey, Mrs. McCabe."

She smiled. "Hey, Mr. McCabe."

"What do you say we go make this family complete?"

She took his hand and they followed the judge out of the room reserved for weddings. Along the way, Jack, who walked with no cane and a hardly notice-able limp, picked up Megan, so pretty in her pink frilly dress. Of course, Tottie was there, too, but now the doll had a full head of brand-new hair and a dress to match Megan's. Of course, the ink hadn't disappeared, but when you love someone, ink doesn't matter.

Then there was Frank, the best man, who looked great after a solid year of recuperation. He'd been wounded in the shoulder, but not too badly. It was just lucky that the paramedics got there when they did, or he might have bled to death. As it was, he was already back at work with his partner. The guys at the department called them the "bull's-eye boys," but it was affectionate respectful teasing.

The best man couldn't seem to keep his eyes off the maid of honor. Crystal, decked out in a red dress that meant business, had become a friend, and as her wedding gift, she'd given Jack his Cadillac.

The whole gang traipsed into the judge's chambers. After Jack put Megan down, he and Hailey each took one of her hands.

The judge, a pleasant woman who had helped them confirm that Megan had no living relatives and that the uncle who'd lived in Oklahoma wasn't blood kin but an ex-cellmate of her father's, looked at Megan and smiled. "Do you know what we're doing here, Megan?"

Megan nodded. "Making Jack my new daddy and Hailey my new mommy."

"Is that what you want?"

Megan nodded again. "Tottie does, too."

"I see."

"And you know what?"

The judge's right brow shot up. "What?"

"I'm going to have a little sister."

"You are?"

She nodded. "Jack promised."

"Well, I think that's just wonderful." The judge signed the papers in front of her, then turned them so Hailey and Jack could sign. Hailey's fingers shook as she put down her new name. Hailey McCabe. It had such a nice ring to it.

Once that was done, Frank kissed her, Crystal hugged her, and Megan lifted her arms so Jack could pick her up.

Hailey turned to the two of them. Her family. Her loves. Her future. "Now what's all this about having a little sister?"

Jack shrugged. "I suppose a little brother would be okay, too."

"I see. And when did you two come up with this brilliant plan?"

"We've been talking about it for weeks," he said.

"And you didn't feel it was necessary to let me in on it?"

"Oh, I intended to," Jack said. "As a matter of fact, I was going to bring it up tonight."

Hailey felt her cheeks heat, but she smiled her pleasure.

Jack looked at her, at his new family. He could still hardly believe it. Faraday was in jail, as were the ex-police captain, Bob Dorran and Brett Nichols. The money-laundering scheme had involved hundreds more, as the notebook had revealed, and even now, a year later, the repercussions were still being felt.

But he didn't pay much attention to that anymore. He was too busy. He still went to the gym five days a week to work out, but his hip was almost as good as new. And then there was all that time he needed to play with Megan. Not to mention, falling more and more deeply in love with his wife. *His wife.*

How a guy like him had lucked out like this was a mystery. One he'd never take for granted.

He'd been given a second chance to live. His kissed his bride, then whispered, ''Thank you.''

HARLEQUIN®

I N T R I G U E®

presents

LOVERS UNDER COVER

Dangerous opponents, explosive lovers—
these men are a criminal's worst nightmare
and a woman's fiercest protector!

A two-book miniseries
by RITA Award-nominated author

Carly Bishop

They're bad boys with badges, who've
infiltrated a clandestine operation. But to
successfully bring down the real offenders,
they must risk their lives to defend the
women they love.

In April 2000 look for:

NO BRIDE BUT HIS (#564)
and
NO ONE BUT YOU coming soon!

Available at your favorite retail outlet.

HARLEQUIN®
Makes any time special™